Married:

Sneaky Black Woman

a novel

by

Antoinette Smith

STTP Books
Riverdale, GA

This is a work of fiction. The names of characters, many locations, and events in this book are fictitious.

Published in the U.S.A. by Straight to the Point Books
Riverdale, Georgia

ISBN: 1-930231-39-3 / 978-1-930231-39-9
Editor: Windy Goodloe
Cover Design: Marion Designs
Interior Book Layout: The Rod Hollimon Company

Printing in the United States of America

From the Twisted Mind of a Gemini

I'm keeping him young was what I thought.
Everything I had, this older man had bought.
Trying to be a young bitch and get away with shit
Was just the beginning of my life I couldn't fix.
Trying to be sneaky and just when I thought I'd gotten away,
He showed me different ways that could end my day.
I knew right from wrong and I should have seen
That I should have been nice to him and not so mean.
But I was blinded by all the money and all the bling.
I had it all from Maybachs to Diamond rings.
Sleeping with a younger man really fucked me up.
Now I'm up the creek and shit out of luck.
Being with an older man was sometimes fun,
Then at times I wanted to just take off and run.
If I knew what I know now back then,
I would never have married his ass back when!!!

Special thanks to El Ranchero Mexican Bar in College Park, GA.
Thank you for letting me sell my books. Robert, George, Nacho,
and Penguin.

Special thanks also to Big Daddy's Catering and Soul Food.

Upcoming Titles by the Author

*WHITE COP LIL BLACK GURL
*I'M A DRAG NOT A FAG
*I'M BI Y LIE?
*BLACK-OUT ON BANKHEAD
*WOMEN R DOGS TOO?
*I WISH I WAS RAISED
*MY LIFE, MY PAIN (BOOK OF POEMS)

*In Remembrance of
my dear friend/Sister
Tremeesa Marquell West*

1
Captain Save-A-Hoe?

Every Saturday morning, I washed my family's clothes at the laundromat. Once I had gotten my twins, Sherita and Shelton, and myself dressed, we all hopped in my '86 Chevy Celebrity. It was a piece of shit. Often, when I was sitting at a red light, I had to throw it into neutral, so it wouldn't cut off.

I lived in the projects with Bernard, my twins' sorry-ass daddy. He never went with us to wash clothes because he knew that my car was unreliable. I hated his nickel and dime ass. He was a poor, hustling, petty-ass drug dealer.

Even though I was young, I had two kids to take care of, and, when it was time for me to go wash clothes, I did just that. I couldn't sit around and wait on Bernard to do anything for us. All Bernard wanted to do was smoke weed and sell drugs out of my apartment. All he did was flip my first of the month check by buying and selling drugs, but, I will say, before I met Bernard, I was in the streets hard. I had to sell my body just to have a place to sleep at night.

It all ended when I met another young girl, who was working on the streets. She told me about the Atlanta Housing Authority. I started getting five hundred dollars in food stamps each month. I remember it like it was yesterday. I went to apply for government assistance, and I got it all. Free food and damn near free rent! My rent was only twenty-two dollars a month, and the utilities were free. We were living it up in the projects.

I tricked off up until I was five months pregnant with my twins. I can't say that I even loved Bernard. He made me so mad at times. The times that I loved him were when he tried to be a daddy to our twins, but that only happened every first of the month.

Old Lady Ethel had given me the car. She lived in the houses that sat outside of the projects. She saw how the twins and I struggled with those black trash bags full of our dirty clothes as we walked to the laundromat.

She said, "Tameka, come on in here. I want to bless you. I want to give you this here car. It isn't much, but you can make it from point A to point B."

I was so happy.

She continued, joking, "As you can see, I have plenty of cars, but I can't drive them all. Plus, when I go to heaven, they sure as hell can't go with me."

Old Lady Ethel had been looking out for me for years. I think she felt guilty because, when my mother died, she had seen it. To this day, I didn't want to know the details. Old Lady Ethel used to run the streets with Twinkie. Twinkie was my mother, but I never called her Mama. I had always called her Twinkie. Her real name was Michelle. She had died many, many years ago, and Old Lady Ethel had tried to look after me ever since, but she had too many rules. That was why I ran to the streets. When I got into trouble, however, she'd still let me shower and eat at her house. Maybe, she felt guilty. I guess, the least she could do was take care of Twinkie's daughter since she claimed to have been there when Twinkie was murdered.

The story that I was told was that Twinkie had stolen millions of dollars from a major drug dealer. I was also told that Old Lady Ethel knew where Twinkie had hidden the money. It still puzzled me, though, and I had a lot of unanswered questions. Why was Old Lady Ethel still alive? Why was my mother dead? Why didn't both of them die together if they were best friends who whored and ran drugs for the same dealer?

Old Lady Ethel said that she had witnessed these so-called drug dealers kill Twinkie, but I didn't believe that. Twinkie's body was never found, so we never had a funeral for her. Everyone just believed what Old Lady Ethel had said — she was killed by crime lords.

Old Lady Ethel and Twinkie weren't your ordinary whores, either. They used to fly to different states and prostitute. Twinkie had it all. Our house was so lavish. Coming up, I didn't want for anything. So, I decided that, as soon as I could, I wanted to have boyfriends just like she'd had. I wanted to moan at night. I wanted my boyfriends to scream my name. My mother was a madam and a pimp. You name it; she did it. I wanted to wear fur, and I wanted to be just like her. Unfortunately, she was a hypocrite. That was why I ran away. Even though I had grown up seeing her with a different man every other night, she had tried to tell me not to have boyfriends, but my curiosity had already been peaked. Hearing her screaming a different man's name every night only increased my interest in her profession.

I missed that lady sometimes, but I had definitely picked up her ways. I was her in the flesh. I didn't take shit from no one, especially those grimy-ass bitches in the projects. I caught my first felony charge when I was eleven. I sliced a bitch from ear to ear, but it was self-defense because about five girls jumped on me over Bernard's ass. They were kicking my ass, but I managed to get my razor out. I sliced one of them, and all of them bitches scattered like roaches.

From that day on, they all spoke to me like we were friends, but I never did trust them. I didn't trust anyone! I didn't even trust myself! I knew Bernard was fucking half of them, but I didn't care. I prayed for a miracle, and I got one. My miracle was Spencer.

When we finished washing at the laundromat, my twins and I piled into my car. I drove a little, but the car stalled. It acted like it wanted to cut off. All the lights on the dashboard blinked off and on. Then, smoke started coming from under the hood. I thought the car was going to blow up! Finally, it just cut off. I pulled over to the side of the road and propped up the hood. I got my twins out and told them to stay put.

They were adorable. They were only five years old at the time, but they were very smart. They stood there, each holding over three garbage bags full of clothes.

I had on my daisy dukes, and I knew someone would stop for me. Like I said, I was Twinkie in the flesh. I looked just like her. We were both chocolate, and we both had big-ass booties. You could see our shape from a mile away.

Finally, a sports car flew past me. Then, it turn around. A tall, older, attractive, well-dressed man got out of the car. He had on a suit, and I saw that his nails were perfectly manicured. He looked foreign. I noticed his eyes first. He had greenish-gray eyes. Cat eyes, if you will. Then, I noticed the cologne he had on. He was wearing Sean John's Unforgivable. I recognized that scent because my brother, George, wore it all the time. *That cologne will make you get naked even if a bum on the street was wearing it,* I thought. It smelled that good!

This man was well-kept, and he was stylish, too. He wore gator shoes with a Steve Harvey three-piece, double-breasted suit. I saw dollar signs.

"What seems to be the problem?" he asked as he approached me.

"This piece of shit-ass car of mine has cut off," I answered as I kicked the door.

"Do you have a name for your car? Sometimes, if we are nice to our cars and call our cars by pet names, they come back to life for us."

"Well, I guess you can call it 'Old Lady Ethel' since Old Lady Ethel gave it to me."

"I want you to put your kids and clothes in my car. Get them away from this street."

"I don't know you like that! I ain't putting them nowhere," I said, looking him up and down.

I sensed that this old man wouldn't harm a fly, but I had to be tough, so he wouldn't think I was scared of him. That was just how you had to be in the streets. The streets had taught me valuable lessons. One of them was, if you act like a pussy, then you will get fucked!

"What is your name?" he asked.

"My name is Tameka," I answered as I blew a bubble with my Hubba Bubba gum.

"Well, Tameka. I am Spencer. Spencer Davis. I will not hurt you or your kids," he said, handing me his business card.

"You look real familiar," I said as I signaled for my twins to get into his fine automobile.

When I got closer to his car, I saw that it was a four-door Porsche and that there were televisions in the headrests.

"Wow!" the twins and I said as I put them in.

"Mommy, can we live in here?" they asked simultaneously.

"Y'all sit here, and don't touch shit. I don't want to have to fuck this old-ass man up, so sit down and watch television."

"Okay, Mommy," they said at the same time.

It was so funny to me when they answered at the same time. I guess that was a twin thing.

I walked back slowly, watching him look under the hood of my car. *I know this man from somewhere, but where?* I thought, but I couldn't put two and two together. He looked old enough to be my daddy or granddaddy. At the time, I was only twenty, and I knew he was, at least, triple my age.

"So, what's wrong with Old Lady Ethel?" I asked sarcastically.

"You have to be good to your car, and your car will be good to you. Cars are like humans. They have feelings, too."

I was waiting for him to say some freaky shit, but he didn't. He was very respectful.

"Your heads are blown. You have water in your oil, and your heads are cracked."

"My what is what? So, what does that mean? Can it be fixed?" I asked.

I didn't know what the hell he was talking about.

"Sure, but, if you try to fix this car, you will have to spend a good grip to get the motor fixed, and getting the motor fixed will cost more than the car is worth."

"So, what are you saying, Spencer?"

"I am saying that this car isn't worth fixing."

"Well, can you drop us off at the top of the projects up the street?"

"Sure. I don't see why that would be a problem. Which ones do you live in — the red ones or the blue ones?

"The red ones," I said with one eyebrow raised.

"Aren't you scared to go in there in this fly-ass car? You might get jacked," I said as we got into his car.

The twins had played themselves to sleep.

"You let me worry about those jack boys," he said as he placed a chrome nine millimeter on the dashboard. "I am from the projects, too. As a matter of fact, I was raised in the blue ones. It's not where you live; it's how you live."

"Well, that's easy for you to say. You don't have to hear gunshots every other night, and you don't have to fight these ghetto-ass bitches every day."

"Well, what are you doing to make your life better?" he asked.

"I just want to be rich. I don't want to work for nobody. I want to live like those rich, white folks I see on television. Most of them don't work! They are born with silver spoons in their mouths."

"So, you want to live like the white folks, huh?"

"No, Spencer. All I'm saying is that I want to leave this ghetto-ass life! I want my kids and me to live comfortable. I have a poor, sorry-ass boyfriend. I want to leave him and get away, you know? I want to get dolled up and be on the cover of a magazine. I have dreams, but I've been told by the people at the welfare office that my attitude will not get me far in life. And I told those bitches not to worry about my attitude and to just give me what the government had promised me! Well, that's enough about me. Tell me about you. Are you a drug dealer or a celebrity? Do you have a wife because I will fight an old-ass lady if I have to? I just don't give a fuck."

"No, I'm not a drug dealer, and I don't have a wife," he chuckled. "You're so feisty. Why are you so defensive?"

"Why am I so what?" I asked as I seductively wrapped strands of my long, black weave around my right index finger.

"You don't have to play tough girl with me," he said. "I am not the enemy here."

"Well, who are you?"

"I'm Spencer. Don't you remember?"

"I mean, are you famous, or what? Because I've seen you somewhere before."

"Just look at me as an angel that God has sent from heaven."

Sometimes, I wish Spencer had kept driving and had never stopped for me.

2
So Long, Bernard

I got Spencer to drop us off at the top of the entrance. I knew, if Spencer had pulled up in front of my building, Bernard would have had a fit.

"You make sure you call me," Spencer said as we got out.

"I'm going to call you tomorrow."

"The sooner, the better," he said before he pulled off.

"Mommy, he looks rich," the twins said.

"He is rich," I said as I stuffed his card in my size Ds.

When we walked in, it seemed Bernard had invited the whole neighborhood into our living room. There was smoke everywhere. The room was filled with the aroma of weed, but the twins and I were used to it because that was all Bernard did — smoke weed and drink Cisco. He and his loser friends were also playing video games. Usually, I would have screamed at his ass, but that never did any good because all he did was beat my ass and fuck me afterwards.

Bernard was tall and skinny with cornrows. He was the first boy that I had ever hooked up with. All the time, I wished I had never fucked him. All the girls were on his jock because he had a car, but he had lost his car a long time ago, fleeing the scene of a roadblock.

His mother lived in the same projects as we did, but she wasn't much of a grandmother to the twins. The only time she came around was to buy drugs from Bernard. Yes, he sold drugs to his own mother. He didn't care. He always said, "Money is money." Bernard was a felon of the state, and he had two strikes. One more strike, and he would be doing time in prison.

"Give me the keys to the car," Bernard said while staring at his video game.

"The car is on the side of the street. It cut off on us."

"What do you mean 'the car is on the street'?"

"The raggedy-ass car broke down, and it wouldn't start back up," I snapped.

The twins and I went to my bedroom and closed the door.

"Mommy, I hate my daddy," Sherita said.

"I hate his ass, too," I replied.

I knew all the answers to all of my prayers had just dropped us off. Even my kids sensed Bernard's bullshit. They had witnessed Bernard beating my ass and giving me black eyes a few times.

I sat both of them on the bed and said, "We're going to run away. We're going to leave this dump, but you can't say anything to Bernard, okay?"

"Your secret is safe with us, Mommy," they both said.

"As soon as I get straight, I'm going to visit Uncle George in jail."

George was my brother, and he was well on his way to doing hard time. He'd been in and out of jail all my life. No matter what, he always made sure to tell me that he loved me, though. He assured me that Twinkie had loved me, too. She had just gotten caught up with the wrong crowd. As far as I was concerned, I didn't need her, anyway. I handled myself on the streets good.

Even though I was ghetto as hell, I had taught my kids to talk different from me. Sherita looked just like Bernard, and Shelton favored me. I loved my kids, and I sure as hell didn't want Sherita selling ass and sucking dick like I'd had to, and I was going to make damn sure Shelton didn't follow in Bernard's footsteps.

"Freeze! Everybody, freeze!"

Suddenly, my apartment filled with men dressed in blue. We were raided by the police. They stormed into my house and locked all them fools up, including Bernard's ass.

"Are you Bernard James White?" one officer asked as he handcuffed him.

"Suck my dick! You don't have nothing on me!"

"Well, what is this?" an officer asked as he flipped over a sofa cushion and pulled out a kilo of cocaine.

My eyes got so big. I didn't even know that Bernard was pushing weight.

"You're wanted in a couple of homicides that took place earlier this week."

"Homicides! Prove it! Those two niggas are dead," Bernard blurted out.

"You're wrong. One of those niggas played dead and identified you as the trigger man before he died at the hospital. You're going to go down for this, and I am so glad I got your bum ass off the streets."

I wasn't shocked, but I knew, if Bernard had killed someone, he wasn't going to see daylight ever again.

"What do we have here?" another officer said, holding up a tech nine.

"Looks like the murder weapon to me," another officer replied.

As they took Bernard and his loser buddies away to jail, Bernard looked at us and said, "Daddy will be home soon."

One of the officers looked at me and said, "You're lucky. You get a pass from Spencer."

"How the fuck does she get a pass? Bitch, did you set me up?" Bernard shouted.

"Hell, no! I didn't set you up. I don't know what's going on."

The twins witnessed their daddy being hauled off to jail. Shelton looked sad, and Sherita cried. I didn't care because I was thinking about Spencer. When we went back into our apartment, it was a mess. The sofas were cut open. Pillow fluff was everywhere. Dishes were broken in the kitchen. I rolled up a joint and called Spencer.

3
Moving On Up

I waited for about a week before going anywhere with Spencer, but, when I did go with him, it was all worth it. Spencer picked us up in a white, four-door Mercedes Benz. I felt all the stares from everyone over there.

"Don't forget where you came from," nosy-ass Old Lady Gladys said from her porch where she sat from sun up to sun down.

I'm going to forget this ghetto-ass place and your worrisome ass, too, I thought.

Spencer stepped out and said, "You can leave everything here because, where we're going, you don't need to bring nothing."

"So, what do you do for a living?" I asked, trying to make conversation.

"All you need to know is that you're in good hands. I am filthy rich."

"How did you get filthy rich? Were you born rich?"

"I am an extremely successful businessman. That is all you need to know."

We rode for a good while until we finally pulled up at a big mansion. My eyes grew big. I'd only ever seen big-ass houses like this on the TV. We entered the grand entrance through French doors.

Who is this man?, I wondered as we walked into his home where the ceilings were never-ending. *Oh, my God,* I thought.

"Can you please remove your shoes?" a maid said with an attitude.

"Bitch, we ain't taking off shit," I said.

"Rita, it's okay. This is Tameka, and those are her twins Sherita and Shelton. They will be living with us," Spencer calmly said. "Can you please show the kids to their rooms?"

"Yeah. You heard him. Show my kids to their rooms."

"Look, Tameka. No need to be hostile here. You asked for peace; you got peace," Spencer said.

"Well, where is our room? I need to take a shower."

"You are so bossy."

"Yeah. I guess you can say that."

When we got to our room, I almost died. The bed was fit for the king that Spencer was. His mansion looked like it could have been on *Lifestyles of the Rich and Famous*. After touring the bedroom, I took a shower. The whole time, I kept thinking that I had hit jackpot. *What is this lonely, old man doing in this big-ass mansion alone? If he has a wife, I don't care. I am going to treat him right*, I thought.

When I got out, Spencer had a robe for me laid out on the bed. He was sitting in his chair, looking at me from head to toe.

"You know you're too pretty to talk the way you do."

"I know, but, sometimes, I have to get rowdy to get my point across."

"Well, you don't have to do any of that here. Rita is my live-in maid, and she's going to be taking care of your twins. So, what I want you to do is apologize to her, okay?"

"Yeah. Whatever."

"All I'm saying is leave that ghetto mentality in the ghetto."

"Okay. I'll apologize to her. So, where is your wife?"

"If you don't ask me about my past, I won't ask you about your past, okay?"

I sure as hell didn't want to tell him that I had fucked every Tom and Dick and Harry to get by, so I said, "Cool. That's a deal."

"Let me show you your new home."

We went to another large room, and he grabbed a remote. Then, a screen came out the ceiling.

"This is some fly shit," I said.

"I will show you the house on this screen."

"What do you mean?"

"I will give you a tour of my house. The whole house will pop up on this wide screen."

I looked at those pictures, and my jaw dropped when I saw that he had a wedding chapel in his damn mansion.

"How much is this place worth?" I asked.

"Forty million," he answered nonchalantly.

"This is a forty million dollar home!" I screamed as I continued to stare at his property on the screen.

My rent was only twenty-two dollars in the projects, and this was worth forty million dollars! This mansion had numerous gardens and an amphitheater and a river out back.

"Is that your bathroom in this house?" I said as I walked to the screen. The sink was twenty-four carat gold, surrounded by royal blue marble, and trimmed in black, and so was the tub!

"Is that a kiddies' swimming pool?"

"No. Don't be silly. That's a jacuzzi."

"A jacu — what?" I asked.

This mansion was like heaven. It even had a nine-hole golf course!

"Mommy! Mommy!" The twins said as they flew in. "Come and see our rooms!"

We all walked to the other side of the mansion.

"Damn! How many bedrooms are in here?" I asked.

"Seventeen," Rita said in her Mexican accent.

Spencer grabbed my hand as we walked down to the twins' rooms. We got to Shelton's room first. It was decked out. He had a Spiderman bedroom suit. He had a PlayStation 3, and there were plenty of clothes and toys throughout. Sherita's room was right next to Shelton's, and it was decked out, too, in black Barbie.

"Is this black Barbie?" I asked as I got closer. "How did you get Mattel to do that?"

"Anything is possible when you have money," he said as he kissed the back of my hand.

She even had a black Barbie laptop.

My kids and I were straight. We had made it out of the projects without a scratch. While standing in Sherita's beautiful, new room, I recalled the times when I used to fight those girls over Bernard's tired ass. When I first had my twins, I used to let another girl come to my house and "play" babysit them. I felt sorry for her because her mother was on drugs, and she had to do whatever she could to get by, but I didn't know was that she was a mother, also. Eventually, she stole all of my twins' clothes. Ever since then, I never allowed any of those bitches back into my apartment. It was crazy over there at times. Generation after generation, it would always be the same. Mothers never encouraged their daughters or sons to go to school. Babies were having babies, so their mothers would never be different. Their lives would never change. They just knew that, if they kept having kids, their government assistance would go up. Now, what kind of example was that? They could have, at least wanted them to be better than they were, but, instead, their daughters fell right in their footsteps. When they got pregnant, they went and sat in the same boat their mothers were already in. All they could do was apply for food stamps and an apartment.

I was glad that I had met Spencer. I had to admit that, sometimes, I wanted to talk proper or correct English. Although I liked slang better, I saw that, with Spencer, I had to change my ways, or we would be going back to the ghetto.

4
Ghetto Habits

I can't lie. When I first got with Spencer, I wasn't used to all the luxury that he had to offer. I had to get used to things, like his huge bed. I was used to sleeping on an air mattress from Wal-Mart. His bed was so huge, and it had decorative pillows all over it.

There was something about him that kind of made me think twice about him, though. He was too quiet, but I didn't care how quiet he was as long as he didn't hurt my kids and me. I was always the one doing all the talking and asking all the questions.

He was a neat freak, too. That was for sure. That mansion was clean from top to bottom. I told the twins that we had to act like we weren't surprised when we saw all the beautiful paintings throughout, but Spencer knew better. He knew we were from the ghetto, and he knew that we hadn't stepped outside of those damn brick walls for one day, but we still put on a good front. We weren't used to taking off our shoes, but we learned quickly. We didn't do that in the ghetto. I had to mop plenty of times with bleach to get that red dirt off those hard-ass floors, and we didn't have a maid to wash dishes. Bernard would pay a crack head to do them from time to time. I'm not saying that I was nasty or anything, but, sometimes, we paid junkies in drugs to clean my apartment. At Spencer's, I felt like I could, finally, really live it up. Now, I was living like them white folks that I saw on television.

One day, I was in the bed, biting my nails, and Spencer walked in and said, "Please stop biting your nails. That's not ladylike."

"Well, I am definitely a lady," I said as I turned over and shook my ass. "I used to get my nails done, but I was always fighting in the projects, so it was just a waste of time. They would break and split my real nails, and that was very painful, so I stopped getting my nails done."

"I want to take you to an upscale spa just up the street from here."

"I'm surprised you don't have one in here. You could put it next to the forty-seat theater room you have."

I went to tell the twins that Mommy would be right back. Sherita was coloring, and Shelton was playing his video game.

"Mommy, look at me shoot these niggas up."

"What did I tell you about that 'n' word?"

"Oh, yeah, Mommy. Look at me shoot these crackers up."

"Now, that's more like it," Spencer said.

My kids were happy, and so was I.

The spa we went to was designed with elegance, and everyone there seemed to know Spencer. He told them what he wanted to have done to me and said he would pick me up in three hours.

"Damn! It's going to take three hours to get my nails did!"

Suddenly, the spa got quiet, and all eyes were on me as I walked in and took a seat. He looked at me, embarrassed, and said, "Sweetie, you're going to get a full body massage, a manicure and a pedicure, and a new hairstyle."

He kissed me on my lips and said, "Enjoy."

I was attracted to him. I loved his eyes and his neatly-trimmed moustache that framed his thick lips.

"Right this way," a short black lady said with an attitude.

As we walked down the hall, I saw other women getting massages. Some were getting their toes done while reading magazines.

"Get undressed," she ordered, throwing a robe at me.

"Undressed? I'm getting my nails done!" I screamed.

"Honey, when you have a man pampering your ass, you better enjoy it while you can, and you better not cheat on Spencer or make him mad, or you will pay the cost," she said.

I felt uneasy about what she said. What did she mean by "don't make Spencer mad"?

"Maybe, you should just mind your fucking business," I mumbled under my breath.

"Larissa will be with you in a moment."

What in the hell can I possibly do in here for three hours?

I wanted to snap on the bitch, but I remembered that Spencer had told me to watch my tongue, but why should I watch my tone if I was a rich bitch now?

Larissa better have an attitude better than your ass, or I'm snapping on her. I don't give a fuck, I thought. I took off my clothes, put on the thick, white robe, and sat in the chair.

I flipped through a magazine that had Paris Hilton on the cover. She looked like she hadn't washed a dish in her life.

"Knock! Knock!" I heard a voice say as the door opened.

"Hello! I'm Larissa, and we're going to give you a full makeover today. You'll get a full body massage by me. Then, you'll get a manicure and a pedicure. Lastly, Jasmine, our top-notch celebrity stylist, will get those tired-ass, crunchy tracks out of your head."

I looked at her and rolled my eyes. I couldn't say anything bad about her because she looked like she had just stepped out of *Jet* magazine, but I could roll my eyes.

"Y'all are not touching my motherfucking weave," I snapped, rolling my neck. "Pooh in the hood hooks me up every other week for twenty-five dollars. You better ask somebody!"

"Wait! Did you say 'twenty-five dollars'? No wonder it looks like you stuck your finger in an electrical socket! I'm just joking," she said quickly. "Can you take a joke?"

I took a deep breath and said, "Well, I do have really long, pretty hair under this, but I like weave better because my real hair always sweats out."

"We got something for that," she said. "Jasmine can lay some real hair. Her work can be seen in this magazine."

Larissa handed me a magazine with Monica on the front. I wanted every style I saw in that book.

Wow! Jasmine is really good, I thought as I flipped through the magazine.

"She can really lay some hair. I would like her to style my hair, especially since Spencer is paying for whatever I want! Larissa, you have a better attitude than that other lady who brought me back here."

"Oh, that's Betty. She's Spencer's sister-in-law."

My heart skipped a beat.

"But Spencer told me he didn't have a wife."

"Well, technically, he doesn't because she went missing some years back. It was all over the news."

Then, a light went off in my head. *That's where I know him from — The Channel Five News.* The headline had read: *Millionaire Mogul Cleared in Wife's Disappearance.*

"Her name was Jo Ann, and Betty believes that Spencer had something to do with her disappearance."

"Well, why did she have an attitude with me? I didn't kill her sister, or make the bitch disappear!"

"So, what's your name?" she asked as she got her things in order.

I nervously said, "Tameka."

I was still stuck on Spencer's wife's disappearance.

"Betty and Jo Ann started this spa together, but, now, Betty runs everything."

"I wouldn't call it a meet and greet; it was more like a scolding."

"She hasn't been right ever since her twin sister went missing."

"They were twins?"

Larissa nodded her head.

"You mean to tell me that God made two of those evil, miserable bitches?"

My heart started beating fast again.

"Well, why did she tell me not to make Spencer mad?"

"Like I said, she thinks he killed her sister, and what can your young ass do with that old-ass, rich man anyway?"

"Excuse me," I said as I rolled my eyes and snapped my neck. "I can do what y'all old hags can't do. I can drop it like it's hot," I said as I dipped to the floor.

"I used to drop it like it's hot back in my days, too. I just don't see how Spencer hooked up with a ghetto tramp like you."

"First of all, bitch, that's MISS GHETTO TRAMP TO YOU! And what is that supposed to mean, lady? You better watch your mouth before I go ghetto on your ass!"

"You're right! I just wish I'd had a chance with Spencer. I don't care if he did kill Jo Ann. I would enjoy that mansion, and I would let him do whatever he wanted to do. That's just how I feel. Any woman in her right mind knows not to cheat on a man that is as powerful as Spencer," she said as she stared off into space.

It took everything in me not to snap on that bitch. I felt like going postal on everyone in that so-called "elegant" spa. Since I had been there, everyone had been staring at me and whispering when they saw me walk by and shit.

"Is that what this is all about? You want my man? Well, bitch, you can't have him! As a matter of fact, send another bitch in here to do my massage. And if the bitch cheated on him, then maybe she got what she deserved!" I screamed before she walked out.

She came back in five minutes later, apologizing and going on about how she needed the money.

"Well, if you need the money, then I suggest you shut the fuck up about my man!"

I agreed to let her finish my massage because I was very tense. I needed my bones rubbed. I laid on the table face down. She poured the hot oil on my back, and her hands were soft. I could have fallen asleep; it felt so good.

"I'm just saying. If I had a good-looking man like Spencer, I would never cheat on him."

"Can you just do your fucking job silently, please?"

But she went on and on about Spencer. I finally jumped up, put on my robe, and stormed out of the room to get my nails done. As I walked down the hall, I heard Betty telling another lady that she had to save that young girl. *She better not be talking about me. I am a grown-ass woman, and I can take care of myself. They're just mad,* I thought. I was so heated and ready to go, but time was moving so slow. I hated being in there with those old bats. I was ready to call Spencer and tell him to come and get me, but he already had this whole day planned out, so I was just going to roll with the punches. Betty walked in and assigned me to another room.

"Just listen to me," she said as she put some champagne on the table.

"You are very outspoken," I said.

"Yes, I am, and I am trying to save your ass because Spencer is a very dangerous man. I know he killed my sister, but I just can't prove it. That's why he brings young, feisty bitches like you in here and pampers you all. He don't have to make things right with me because my sister was good to him, but he started cheating and beating on her. She would show me bruises from him grabbing her and throwing her around. I remember the late night phone calls I used to get from my sister about all of the affairs she witnessed him having. I know Spencer, and he is up to no good."

"Well, he's not going to beat my ass because I have the goods to keep his old ass in line. I am a big girl. I know how to get and keep a man. Besides, I am grown, and Spencer wouldn't hurt a fly."

She said, "Don't say I didn't try to warn you."

She poured me a tall glass of champagne.

"Now, this is more like it," I said as I gulped it down like a forty.

"You don't have any class, do you?" she said as she poured me another glass. "Do you know how to sip on a three hundred dollar bottle of champagne? You're supposed to sip slowly; it's not going anywhere."

"No, I'm actually trying to get drunk, so I don't have to pay you bitches no mind before I go off on one of y'all in here."

"Where is your mother? Does she have any class?"

That was it. I jumped on her old ass, and all of the employees had to get me off of her.

"Why in the hell did Spencer bring me to this place?" I screamed.

"He brought you here to show me that he could have other bitches after my sister. He wants to rub my face in it."

Then, a nail tech came and took me to the stylist's side of the spa.

"You're going to be dead next," Betty said as the nail tech and I walked down the hall.

Jasmine walked in and introduced herself, and she asked me how I wanted my hair done. I told her I wanted my hair styled the way she had done Monica's on the April cover of *Essence* magazine.

Jasmine was very pretty. She was tall and dark brown, and she looked like a super model. Her teeth were pearly white, and she had her hair laid. Her side of the spa was hooked up. It was decorated with white leather sofas with black leather pillows and black and white spiral lamps throughout. It looked like a VIP area in an exotic night club. She played various R & B slow jams. She didn't talk much because she was all about her business, and her business was hair. I sipped on a little more champagne and called Spencer to come and pick me up when she was done. By the time I left there, I looked like I needed to be on the cover of a magazine.

5

A Night on the Town

When Spencer arrived, he was in a stretch Cadillac limo, and he stood outside, holding a bouquet of red roses. *All this for a little ghetto girl,* I thought. I wanted to bring up Jo Ann, but that wasn't the time, and, besides, we had agreed to leave our pasts in the past.

"You look like a million bucks," he said as he opened the door for me.

"Thanks to you, daddy," I said as I rubbed him between his legs.

In the streets, I learned that tricks loved for me to call them daddy, but that wasn't the case with Spencer because he was a different breed.

"I've never been in a limo before. This motherfucker is fly! Is this Hennessey? This is my drink," I said as I held up the bottle. "What the fuck are you looking at?" I asked the driver.

"You don't have any class or manners, do you?" Spencer said.

"So, what the fuck are you trying to say, Spencer? What do you expect? I've been in the streets since I was thirteen. Hell! The streets practically raised me," I said as I popped the top on the Hennessey.

At that point, I didn't care what anyone thought of me. I was living in a forty million dollar mansion.

"All I'm saying is, baby, I know it's not easy to leave that hell hole and come to the rich life, but you have to start acting like you have some type of class. You have to stop cursing people out, and you have to sit with your legs crossed, and you have to stop biting your nails. You have to remain a lady at all times."

"Well, what do you expect from a girl who raised herself?" I screamed. "Are you going to put me in an etiquette school next?"

"I have a lot in store for you," he said as he snapped his fingers, signaling for his driver, Q, to drive off.

"Spencer, I never ever want to go to that salon again. That Betty bitch made me feel small. Oops! Am I being ghetto again? Let me rephrase that. Betty made me feel small. She kept saying that you had killed her sister, and Larissa wanted me to practically give you to her! I didn't know what to think, and why did you take me there out of all the salons and spas in the Atlanta? Your wife left you, right? I mean you're not a killer, are you?" I asked, being very serious.

"No! Don't be silly," he chuckled. "Just leave the past in the past."

Something in my gut was telling me to leave him, but there was no way I could leave all that money.

"But I do want Jasmine to continue to do my hair, but not there at the salon."

"I will arrange for Jasmine to do your hair at the mansion. Hell! I'll even offer Jasmine her own salon," he joked.

I saw the driver watching me through the rearview mirror. Spencer snapped his finger for the driver to roll up the partition window. I laid on Spencer's chest. I felt like he was my guardian angel. How hard is it not to cheat when you're rich?

"Can you buy me a Maybach?"

"Sure, baby. You can have whatever you want. Just don't make me mad."

Chill bumps grew all over my body when he said that because all I could do was think about Betty saying, "Don't make him mad, or you'll pay with your life."

I didn't know what the hell a Maybach was. I just knew it was a fly car because the rapper Rick Ross, talked about it in his rap songs.

I could have everything. All I had to do was obey him. How hard was that?

When we finally stopped, we were at Phipps Plaza.

"Look, Spencer. I'm not wearing no old-ass lady clothes. Oh, my bad! I'm sorry. Am I being ghetto again?"

He didn't have to answer because, if looks could have killed, I would have been dead. He cleared his throat and said, "This is my Black Card. I want you to use it to get a sexy dress. We're going somewhere special tonight. I want you to look sexy. I want you to look lovely. I have people I want you to meet."

"How much can I spend?" I asked.

"The sky is the limit," he said. "Now, go have fun. I'll be back in two hours."

Wow! I had never seen a Black Card before. The only card I had was a damn food stamp card, and that only had food stamps on it and two hundred and eighty dollars cash for the twins.

When I was riding up the escalators, I saw all kinds of people. I had never been to Buckhead before. It looked like Hollywood. Everyone had on big shades, and they were carrying numerous shopping bags.

The first store I went in was Gucci. I spotted a pair of shades that I liked, so I tried them on. I wanted some big shades to cover my eyes, too. I often referred to them as hater blockers.

"May I help you?" a tall, white, female sales associate asked. "My dear, those shades are fifteen hundred dollars each. Maybe you should go to the flea market and get a knockoff pair for five bucks."

"Bitch, I have a Black Card," I said as I held it up. "That's what y'all crackers get. Always thinkin' a nigga can't afford shit. As a matter of fact, give me three pairs. I want a brown, silver, and black pair. I also want two pairs of those boots in the corner in black and red in a size eight."

"I'll need to see some identification," she said before realizing Spencer's name was on the front of the Black Card. "Oh, Spencer Davis is a loyal customer of ours. Are you his daughter or his niece?"

"No! I'm his fucking girlfriend! Any more questions, Ms. Kincaid?" I said as I read her name tag. "And make sure the black guy in the back gets the commission."

I was having a *Pretty Woman* moment.

"You told me to go to the flea market. You got some fucking nerve. You better make sure he gets the commission, too. I will call up here and ask for the manager to see if he gets it, too."

"I will certainly see to it that he gets it," she said as she slid the Black Card through the terminal.

"You better," I snapped. "Try me. I'm from the hood, and I know people that will make your skinny, prissy ass disappear!"

"Will you make me disappear just like Spencer's ex-wife did ten years ago?"

"What did you say? Speak up! I didn't think so," I said as a put on a pair of my fifteen hundred dollar Gucci shades.

"Have a wonderful day, and please come to Gucci again," Ms. Kincaid said.

"You better be nice to me next time, and, trust me, there will be a next time. No need to try and suck up to me now," I said as I grabbed my bags and left.

The next stop was Versace. I didn't know anything about these famous designers. All I knew was that I had watched stars like Halle Berry and Beyoncé wear their clothes and shoes on the red carpet. I didn't have to be a star, but, as long as I was with Spencer, my twins and I were going to live like stars.

"May I help you?" a short black girl asked. "I'm Bianca, and I am here to help you with anything you need today."

She was brown-skinned with neat, short dreads. I noticed that she was wearing Unforgivable by Sean John. I was glad she didn't judge me like everyone else I had come in contact with so far that day. *Now, that's customer service,* I thought as I glanced at the gorgeous gowns.

"I want this dress that's on this mannequin. I want to see one in blue, black, and red."

"Sure. No problem. What size do you need?" she said as she focused her eyes on my butt.

"I need a size five or six."

"These sizes here start at extra small and go up to large. To me, you look like you're a medium," she said, looking at my waistline.

"And I'll take those stilettos, too, in a size eight in black and red."

"I'll meet you in the dressing room," she said as she went to get the dresses.

After five minutes, we were in the dressing room. I was preparing to try on the beautiful dresses.

"Here we are. Shall we try it on?" Bianca said.

"Sure. Why not? I have to make sure all of this ass can fit. Well, are you just going to stand there? Help me!" I snapped.

She had been daydreaming, staring at my body.

"Oh, yes! Sure. I can help," she stuttered. "Here. Careful," she said as she helped me pull off my sweater. "We don't want to mess up that pretty hair."

Jasmine had given me a razor cut bob.

"Hell, no!" I said. "My man is taking me somewhere special tonight."

I slipped off my clothes and slipped on the black dress first. It hugged every curve on my body.

"This is a Kodak moment," Bianca said.

She left out the dressing room and returned with a Kodak digital camera.

"Say cheese!"

"Cheese," I said as I hammed it up. "Oh, my God! I look so good!"

"Mind if I take one with you?" she asked as she eased next to me.

She came closer, and we put our faces together, and she snapped the shot.

"You smell really good," she said.

"No. You're the one who smells good. I love that Unforgivable cologne."

"How did you know? Oh, I forgot that you have a man," she said with a frown. "What kind do you have on?"

"This is Be Delicious by Donna Karan. This is my favorite. I wear this every day!"

"Perfect," she said as she showed me the pictures.

"Whoop! There it is," I said. "I look better than them damn people on television."

"You sure do," she whispered. "Is there anything else I can get for you?"

"This will be all," I said as I began to get dressed.

I realized that I would have to change my tone for Spencer and his rich friends that night. I didn't want to embarrass him. I couldn't wait for him to see the gowns that I had picked out. Once I arrived at the register, Bianca had already added my things up. The grand total was thirteen thousand. Oh, well! He said there was no limit and for me to get whatever

I liked! I handed her the Black Card, and she swiped it. She didn't even look at it. She was too busy flirting with me.

"I'm new in town, and I'd love to hang out with you," she said as she gave me my card and receipt. "I live in a loft around the corner, and I haven't met anyone, yet."

We exchanged numbers, and I left, so I could continue my shopping spree. By the time I left, I had spent thirty grand.

6
Family Ties

When Spencer picked me up, he had let the sunroof back on his black Bentley coupe. *How many cars does he have?*, I wondered. He was playing "Cruising" by Smokey Robinson.

"Hey, baby," I said as I threw my bags in the back.

I kissed and hugged him so tight. I was so happy that I had met him.

"Did you get everything you wanted?"

"About that," I nervously said. "I spent—"

He cut me off, saying, "Don't worry about it. As a matter of fact, that is your card. Keep it for you and the twins."

I sat back in the seat and listened to Smokey blow. Spencer held my hand as we drove through the Buckhead traffic. When we arrived back at Spencer's mansion, we entered on the side of the seven-car garage.

"I haven't been on this side before," I said as we drove down the tree-lined driveway.

"I am also a gun collector," he said as he pointed to the walls once we got out of the car.

The walls in the garage were covered with virtually every firearm known to man. From a three-eighty back up to an AK-47. *I will never do anything to piss him off for sure*, I thought. When we walked into the house, Rita informed us that the twins had played themselves to sleep.

"We had a ball! We watched movies, ate popcorn, and played Twister," she explained.

"Thanks, Rita," I said, remembering that Spencer had wanted me to apologize to her. I planned on apologizing, but I wanted to do it when I felt like it.

"No problem. They're like my kids, now," Rita said.

Spencer and I went into our separate bathrooms. His room included his and her bathrooms. *I must be special,* I thought as I ran my bubble bath and looked around the elegant bathroom. It was the size of a bedroom. It was so big and roomy. When I got out to dry off, Spencer had already put on a black Armani suit with a red tie. He also put on a red brim.

"Wow! You look like you could be my pimp. Those gator shoes you have on are very fly."

I slipped on my black Versace dress and the heels to match. He threw on a splash of Unforgivable, and I sprayed on some Be Delicious. We were both ready for the world. I knew I didn't know what he was up to, but, as long as he didn't harm me, I was cool. I couldn't believe that he hadn't tried to fuck me, yet. Every time I tried to rub on his dick, he would move my hand out of the way. Sometimes, I wondered if he had a dick. I had been pleasuring myself with toys, but that would only last temporarily.

We didn't ride in the Bentley that night. Instead, we rode in his white on white BMW 750. I sat back and listened to the words of Johnnie Taylor's "It's Cheaper to Keep Her". All I could do was think about Spencer's ex-wife, who no one had heard from in ten years.

We pulled up to a huge mansion that looked similar to Spencer's.

"This is my sister Evelyn's place."

"Your sister?" I asked, confused.

He had never spoken of any relatives. Hell! He hardly ever talked.

"Evelyn is my baby sister, but she acts like she's older than me."

"Where are your parents?" I asked.

I knew they were probably dead because he was sixty.

"My parents are deceased," he said as he took off of his seatbelt.

"My mother is dead, too, so don't feel bad, and I never knew my daddy," I said.

"Now, sweetie, when we get in there, you have to stay close by because you could get lost."

"No problem, baby," I said as we headed for the door.

There were security cameras all around.

When we entered, his sister greeted us at the door.

"Hello," she said with the fakest smile ever.

He introduced me as his tenderoni. I extended my hand to shake hers, but she said, "Baby, I don't shake hands, but it's nice to meet you." Then, she turned to her brother and said, "You got yourself a young one this time."

She looked me up and down. I didn't care if she liked me or not. She wasn't the one that I was going to be fucking.

While we sat in the family room, I noticed that there were pictures on the wall of an attractive boy.

"Eric, get in here!" Evelyn shouted. "Your favorite and only uncle is here!"

"I'm on my way in there!" Eric shouted back.

"I will catch up with you guys later," Evelyn said before she left.

When Eric walked in, we instantly locked eyes. He was so handsome. He was tall and brown-skinned with a baby face, and his eyes were grayish blue. His hair was curly and cut in a temp fade. He looked like he was an NBA player because he was tall with an athletic build. I saw his six-pack through the tank top that he had on with a pair of Jordan gym shorts. I don't know why, but I focused on his dick. I saw the imprint of his dick through his gym shorts.

"This is Eric, my smart and talented nephew. He is seventeen, and he's already been asked to play basketball for several of the top ten colleges in the U.S. He will be in the NBA soon. Nephew, this is my soon-to-be-wife Tameka."

"I see that you get your looks from your handsome uncle," I said.

He started blushing, and I knew he was feeling me because I was feeling him. As I was taking in his nephew, Spencer's cell phone rang. It was constantly ringing.

"Sweetie, I have to go handle some business. My nephew will take good care of you until I get back."

Spencer practically ran out the door.

"So, what the hell is a fine-ass bitch like you doing with my old-ass uncle? I know you only want him for his money."

"What young bitch wouldn't?" I replied. "Besides, he's good to my twins."

"Twins?" he replied. "Damn! Turn around. Twins came out of that fat ass?"

He turned me around and looked at my ass.

"I know my uncle can't tap that ass like I can," he said as he continued to spin me around, checking out my goods. "You need a young nigga like me to hit that pussy because my uncle can't do anything for you."

He's right, I thought, *because Spencer hasn't even seen my pussy.*

"Do you have any vodka?" I asked, trying to change the subject.

"Baby, we got whatever you want. Follow me," he said as he led the way to the bar area.

He was right. We went to a room where there was a full-sized bar. I wanted to have a sip of everything.

"You may as well kick them shoes off and get comfortable because my uncle will be gone for a while."

"How do you know?"

"I just know because my uncle is always busy. So, do you want that vodka on the rocks, or do you want a chaser?

Chasers are for suckers," he added as he took a shot of Grey Goose.

"Well, since you put it like that, give me a double shot."

And the more I drunk, the looser I got, and I remember thinking, *Either Spencer is going to fuck me, or I am going to fuck Eric.* I kicked off my shoes and put my legs up on the sofa. Eric came over and massaged my feet.

"That feels so good. I like an affectionate man."

He then came closer and kissed me. I wasn't shocked because I knew I was going to kiss him sooner or later. I just wanted him to make the first move. My pussy instantly got wet. I was ready to fuck.

"Why is your underage ass drinking?"

"Because I am rich and I can. I got money. I got power, and I got the respect out here in the streets."

"Yeah, right,' I said. "I bet you don't even know what the hood looks like while you're talking about the streets respect you. Who are you?"

"I'll show you who I am. Follow me."

We walked down to the other side of the mansion, and we entered his room. He had posters of Michael Jordan covering his wall. My head was starting to spin, and I was definitely feeling the vodka. He turned on his stereo, and I jumped up and danced to the reggae beat. I was winding my hips like those girls in the Sean Paul videos. He came behind me, and I felt his dick on my ass. My pussy was hot, and I was ready to be fucked. He turned me around, and his hand disappeared under my dress. His fingers slid in and out of my pussy.

"I want to feel you inside me," I said as I opened my legs wider, "but not here. What if someone catches us?"

"No one is going to catch us, and, besides, look at all of these cameras. We can see the front gate," he said as he took off his tank top.

He then pressed a button on the remote. I licked his chest and sucked on his nipples. I felt his dick poking me in my stomach.

"What the hell am I doing? Eric, what are we doing?" I asked as I took his dick out of his shorts.

"We're doing what we want to do."

He sat on the edge of a chair and motioned for me to come over.

"Can you give me some head?" he bluntly asked. "I like getting my dick sucked."

"Game recognizes game," I said as I took off my panties and balled them up in my hand.

"What do you mean, baby?"

The sound of him calling me "baby" sounded so good to me. I knelt down to suck his big dick. I couldn't believe that I had my man's nephew's dick in my mouth. He smelled so good. He had even sprayed Unforgivable on his dick, and the thought of him being a ball player turned me on even more. His dick was so hard, and I sucked it so good that he screamed my name. Then, he switched up and said, "Baby, please make slurping sounds. Let me know that you're enjoying sucking my dick."

I started slurping his dick like I was slurping on a snow cone.

"I could slurp and slob on your dick all night," I said as I kept on slurping.

His dick was harder than frozen pig feet. He stopped me and said, "Baby, come on up here and ride this dick."

"Where is your rubber?"

"Aren't you on the pill?"

"No, I am not, but, lucky for you, I got my tubes tied."

When I was in the streets, I never fucked without a rubber. You couldn't pay me to, and those tricks were paying.

"You're only seventeen. How many hoes could you have fucked already?" I said as I jumped on his dick.

"Yeah, that's it," he whispered. "That's how I like it. I like for my woman to take charge of this dick."

"You're a little boy. What are you doing with this big-ass dick?" I said as I sucked on his ears.

He was sweating, and I was licking him everywhere. His sweat tasted so damn sweet.He put my breasts together and started licking them at the same time. That made my pussy get even wetter. I was about to explode on his dick. I was riding his dick harder, and he was screaming my name louder and louder, so I put my panties in his mouth.

"Is this how you like it?" I whispered in his ear.

"Hell, yeah, baby! I'm about to nut all in that pussy."

I looked in his eyes, and I saw that he was about to cum. I was fucking him hard then slow. Then, I felt his body go limp, but I was still hunching because his dick was still hard. Finally, I was out of gas, but we started kissing again, and I was ready for round two.

"I want to see more of you," he said as he looked at the security monitor to the main gate.

"I don't think that's a good idea."

"Well, that's too bad," he said as he grabbed my cell phone and dialed his number. "We already did it. Plus, he's never going to find out," he assured me.

He grabbed his cell phone and saved my number. Then, he said, "Now, that's my number. You can put me up under 'Jody'."

"Why 'Jody'?" I asked.

"Because Jody is a man that pleases a woman when her man can't. Oh, shit! There goes my uncle," he said as he put on his shorts.

My heart was racing.

"I told you we were going to get caught."

"We're not getting caught," he said as he pressed the remote.

I slipped on my panties. I didn't even have time to wash up. I ran to the family room, sat on the couch in there, and pretended to flip through the pages of a random magazine. I didn't see where Eric went. Spencer walked in and said, "I'm sorry, sweetheart, but I had to take care of some very important business. You understand, don't you?"

"Sure. I understand. You're a businessman."

Eric came flying in with a basketball to make it look like he had been on the court shooting hoops.

"Unk, you finally made it back. I was on the court getting my hoops on. You know I got to stay fit for the try-outs."

"That's right, nephew. You keep practicing those jump shots."

Wow! He lied better than me. I couldn't believe Spencer didn't suspect anything. When we got in the car, Spencer continued to apologize for having left me alone for so long. I didn't want to hear anything. I just wanted to jump in the tub.

"I have a surprise for you, baby, when we get home."

"I like surprises," I said, trying to sound like I was interested in his conversation.

I couldn't get Eric's face out of my mind when he was about to cum, especially his facial expression and his deep dimples. I wanted to hook up with him again. That was for sure. *That boy has a nice size dick on him*, I thought as I sat back in the car. I felt kind of bad for fucking Spencer's nephew, but the damage had already been done. I felt something warm coming out of my pussy. I knew it was Eric's cum.

7

Spencer, Not Now

When we got back to Spencer's place, I knew he had sex on his mind. I could tell.

"Come on, my sweetness. Let me carry you to the bed," he said, picking me up. "I have a special treat for you tonight. I wasn't able to take you out like I planned, so I'll make it up in the bedroom."

I wanted to just go to sleep, but he had other things in mind. I laid down, thinking, *If I acted like I was sleepy, maybe he'd let me go to sleep.* Of all nights, why would he want to have sex tonight?

"I'm going to take a shower. I'm sweaty."

"No, you're fine," he said, throwing me on the bed.

He ripped off my dress like he was looking for something. The more he grabbed and tussled me, the more I thought about Eric's cum seeping out of my pussy. He snatched my panties off and dove between my legs face first. It was too late to stop him. He was down there, eating me like endless shrimps at Red Lobster.

"I know how to make that pussy wet," he said as he continued to eat me out. "I'm from the old school. I know how to make a woman feel good. How does that feel, baby?"

"It feels good," I lied.

I couldn't even concentrate on catching a nut with him. The thought of him licking and swallowing Eric's cum made my flesh crawl. *Oh, what the hell,* I thought. *I did crazier shit when I was whoring in the streets.* He really thought that he was the reason that I was soaking wet, so I said, "Yes, baby. You do know how to make me feel good."

I wanted him to think that he was doing something. Eric was the young one with a grown man's dick. I just laid there, irritated, as he nibbled and slurped on my clit. I wanted him to finish quickly. The vodka had worn off, so all I had was the high of my memories with Eric, so I continued to think about Eric. I imagined that it was Eric eating my pussy, not Spencer. I started moaning and faking like I was about to cum.

"Oh, baby. Right there. I'm about to cum."

This wasn't the first time that I'd faked an orgasm. How would he know? I had yet to feel what Spencer's dick felt like. I could do this all day— fake orgasms and go on shopping sprees. What a life? What more could my ghetto ass ask for?

Spencer rose and, as I was about to return the favor, he moved me out of the way. I was glad because the only dick I wanted to suck was Eric's. I got up and ran myself a nice, steaming hot bubble bath. What the hell was I thinking having sex with my man's nephew? I was feeling guilty and slutty, but I thought back to how, in the streets, I'd slept with different men all the time, so that shouldn't have mattered, either.

It was too late. The damage had already been done. I couldn't help but think about how Eric had my pussy throbbing. Why did I have these feelings for him so quickly? I guess it was because I loved the way he talked to me while I was riding his dick. I loved looking into his colorful eyes. I was scrubbing between my legs to get that mixture of Eric's cum and Spencer's slob out from down there. I just hoped Eric could keep our little secret quiet because I wasn't going to tell a soul. When I came back in the room, Spencer was sitting in his chair, smoking a Cuban cigar.

"You look like an angel," he said as he spun in the chair to face me.

"That's a first. Bitch is practically my middle name. I've never been called an angel before," I said as I sat on his lap.

"That's because you've been with the wrong men. I am a real man, baby, and I want you to marry me. Will you marry me?" he asked as he handed me a small jewelry box.

I opened it up and, inside, found the biggest diamond ring that I had ever seen!

"Is this real?"

"Now, what kind of question is that? Look around you. Everything in here is real."

"Hell, yeah! I will marry your ass. I am tired of going to the welfare office, applying for food stamps and shit."

"I need to know that you will never cheat on me or lie to me."

"I won't cheat on you, Spencer. I have everything a girl could want."

"Let's get some rest, baby. We have a long day ahead of us tomorrow," he said as he carried me to his double king-sized, pillow-topped bed.

8
Our Special Night

We awoke to a wonderful aroma and found that Rita had fixed an old country style breakfast that included everything from steak omelets to hot-buttered cheese grits.

"You know Rita is the reason I am in such good shape. She knows how to cook the healthiest food for an old man like me."

I looked over at Rita. Then, I quickly looked at the twins because I didn't want them to catch me mean mugging her. There was something not right about her, too. I had a feeling that she was up to something, but I didn't know what.

"Rita, I want you to take the kids out shopping and to the park. Buy them what their tiny hearts desire," Spencer said.

"Do you guys like Six Flags?" Rita asked the twins.

"Yeah!" my twins replied.

I was so happy that my twins were happy. When they were happy, I was happy; when they were sad, I was sad.

"Have fun," I said as I hugged and kissed them both.

"We love you, Mommy!"

"I love you, too," I said to them. Then, turning to my fiancé, I said, "So, Spencer, when are we getting married?"

I cut open my homemade biscuit and poured some maple syrup on it.

"Are we getting married at the wedding chapel here at the mansion? I am ready to have that thing on my head and over my eyes."

"It's called a veil," Rita interjected.

"Well, yeah. That," I said as I rolled my eyes at her.

"Soon, my dear, soon," he said as he took a cocktail of colorful pills.

"Are you getting high at the table? What are those pills you're taking?"

"Those are his herbal vitamins that keep him fit and healthy," Rita said as she cleared the table.

"So, what do you have planned for us today?" I asked Spencer.

"Oh, a little bit of this and a little bit of that, but, first, I have a surprise for you. Close your eyes," he said as he grabbed my hand.

"Where are we going?"

"It's a surprise. If I tell you, then it won't be a surprise, okay?"

He led me all the way to his seven-car garage. Finally, he said, "You can open your eyes now."

I opened my eyes and saw a black two-door coupe car in front of me. It was shiny, and the rims were red.

"What's this?" I asked.

"This is the Maybach."

Wow! I thought. I wanted to ride through the ghetto and let them raggedy bitches smell my new car. My car probably smelled better than their roach-infested apartments.

"You mean to tell me you asked for a car that you have never seen before? This car was sent in from Berlin just for you."

"Oh! I have seen it before. I lied."

"My favorite colors are black and red, and that's why I had this specially made. This is a Maybach Exelero. You see I had it custom-made, and it's equipped with a surround sound stereo and diamond-quilted, black leather seats with red seatbelts. You have to be very careful when you drive it because this car has 700 horsepower, and it goes up to three hundred and fifty miles per hour. It has a V12 engine, so you do not have to floor the gas pedal. The two M's on the front of it are an acronym for 'Money Meka'. I want to give you whatever makes you happy. Now, let's go inside and get ready for our day."

I walked away, feeling like I was in a dream. I was waiting for someone to pinch me, so I could wake up and see that we were still in the projects, but Spencer was definitely a man of power, and I loved that about him. Everywhere I went, his name rang bells in people's ears. Spencer had our whole day planned out. We were going to the aquarium, to a nice candlelight dinner, then to his friend's jazz bar. I didn't care for jazz, but, if he wanted me to be his eye candy in the club, I was with that.

We arrived downtown at the aquarium, and I wasn't amused at being surrounded by glass and water full of fish. What if the glass cracked and all those fish ate us? I always thought crazy stuff like. No matter what, I always expected the unexpected. As we watched the sharks swim freely in the blue water, I felt all the stares from all the other people. I knew what they were thinking, *What is that young girl doing with that old man?*

I saw this young white couple look at me and smile. Why did they do that? For some reason, white people always had a confused smirk on their faces when they looked at Spencer and me. They'd always smile at me like shit was funny.

Spencer had warned me about acting ghetto in public, so I just ignored them and kept watching the many species of fish. We left there, and we went to an upscale restaurant in North Atlanta. When we arrived in my new Maybach, all of the valets ran to the car when they noticed that Spencer was driving.

"I tip good," he said as he pulled up. "Some of these guys depend on my tips to pay half their rent."

As we got out of the car, he said to the valets, "Today, all ten of you guys are lucky. I am in a very good mood. Therefore, I will give you all a one hundred dollar tip."

"You have a lovely daughter," one of them blurted out.

"This isn't my daughter. She is my new love."

The one that had spoken looked very confused. He walked away, scratching his head. I felt all eyes on me when we walked in, and I enjoyed the attention. Spencer led me to a private seating area that was occupied by only one other couple. There were bottles of wine and cognac on the table. Candles were lit, and there were shiny, gold curtains separating us from everyone else.

"I want you to meet my buddy," Spencer said as he opened the gold curtain that separated us from the other couple.

The man stood up and hugged Spencer.

"You must be the new bride-to-be," he said as he kissed the top of my hand.

"Yes, she is. This is Tameka. She's my sweet tenderoni."

I observed his lady out the corner of my eye, looking at me.

"Tameka, this is my best friend Walter, and this is our friend Janet," Spencer said.

She cracked a fake smile as she eyed me from head to toe. I was looking good because I had on a silk, emerald blue Versace dress. I was up on the hottest styles because I frequently surfed the net, looking at the latest fashion.

"How do you do?" she asked as she extended her right hand towards me.

"Lovely," I said with fakeness.

I wanted her to know that I could be fake, too. *These people are too much for me*, I thought as I sat down.

"You two make a great couple, so when is the big day?" Walter asked.

"Sooner than she thinks," Spencer said as he kissed me on the lips.

I felt stares from Janet, but I didn't care. Why do black women envy other black women on the spot? I mean she didn't know me from a can of paint, but she was already giving me dirty looks. She was cute for her age, though. She looked like she might have been a bad bitch, like me, back in her day.

Walter looked like money, too. I wondered what he did for a living.

"Sweetheart, this lovely restaurant belongs to Walter," Spencer said.

"Of course, if it wasn't for you, I would have gone under years ago," Walter intervened.

"That's what friends are for," Janet said as she looked at Spencer and winked.

Now, I know you just didn't wink at my man in my face, bitch. I may be young, but I will kick your ass, I thought.

"Sweetie, I am going to the men's room. I will be back shortly," Spencer said.

Good, I thought. *This is my chance to flirt with Walter.*

"This is a nice place," I said as I looked around, admiring all the nice VIP booths with red leather sofas and the Jamaican tri-colored lamps.

"The decorations were Janet's idea. She has excellent taste."

At that moment, Janet's phone rang.

"Baby, I have to take this," she said as she answered her phone and left.

"So, Walter, are you a millionaire, too?" I asked as I opened my legs slowly for him to notice that I didn't have on any panties.

"That depends on what you call a 'millionaire'," he answered as he stared at my Mohawk shaved pussy.

"Do you have a big mansion like we got?" I asked.

I closed my legs because I only wanted to give him a sneak peek.

"Yes, I do have a mansion. As a matter of fact, it's three streets over from Spencer's."

"Is that right?" I said as I sipped on some champagne slowly. Then, I asked, "So, is Janet your wife or girlfriend?"

"Janet is actually a childhood friend who attended school with Spencer and me. She's going through a breakup, so I invited her out to have some fun with us."

"Did you like what you saw between my legs?" I boldly asked as I licked my lips.

"You shouldn't do an old man like that," he said as he loosened his Steve Harvey neck tie. "You are engaged to my best friend."

"What he don't know won't hurt him," I said as I straightened my back, which forced my breasts to thrust forward. They almost popped out of my dress.

"Now that I think of it, Spencer took my high school sweetheart from me. Jo Ann was her name," he said as he drifted off into space.

"Jo Ann," I repeated. "You mean the Jo Ann that's been missing for the past ten years?"

"It was more like puppy love, but I cared deeply for her."

"If you want to get even, then here I am."

"Is this a joke? Do you really expect me to sleep with my best friend's girl?"

"Hell, yeah! Didn't he do it to you?"

"Yes, he did, but I forgave him. Plus, he's been so good to me."

"Look! I get what I want. If you don't want this sweet, black pussy, then I will throw it somewhere else. Besides, you said you were rich, so what could possibly happen?"

"He could kill me! That's what could happen! Hell! He could kill both of us."

"Suit yourself," I said as I poured myself another cup.

Spencer and Janet returned at the same time. Janet whispered something in Walter's ear and proceeded to leave. She, then, hugged Spencer and said a weak-ass good-bye to me.

"I am getting kind of hungry, Spencer. I don't need a fancy menu, either," I said as I looked at Walter. I already knew what I had a taste for.

"What does your little heart desire?"

Deep down inside, I wanted to say Eric's dick, but I would have been out of line.

Instead, I said, "I would like a nine-ounce rib eye steak with seasoned broccoli and some rice pilaf."

Spencer snapped his fingers to catch the attention of a waitress walking by. He ordered my food and gave her a nice tip up front.

"You know you don't have to tip them that much money."

"I tip them well because I insist on excellent service. What the hell does it matter, anyway? When I die, I can't take all of my money with me. I look at life like this — you can never share too much money, and you can't ever find a better friend than yourself. You know the saying, 'It's better to give than to receive', right?" Spencer said.

Walter didn't look my way anymore for the rest of the night. *Why am I like this?* I wondered. I have everything I could possibly want. Why did I fuck Spencer's nephew, and why was I now flirting with his best friend? I guessed that I was just immune to monogamy. I didn't care, and it didn't matter to me as long as I got what I wanted, and I didn't get hurt. I just didn't give a fuck. Maybe, I was Twinkie's daughter after all? She'd had it all. Why couldn't I have it all? She'd had more than enough, and I witnessed it up until I was thirteen years old. It was almost like my heart turned cold when I started selling my body on the streets.

"How many forks do I need to eat with?" I asked as I looked at the silverware.

"This is your cocktail fork, and this is your salad fork," the waitress said as she held them in the air one by one.

"Well, I didn't order a salad, and I only need one to eat with. Thank you very much."

Walter looked at me and shook his head. Spencer didn't do anything but sit there because he was used to my outspoken ass.

"Just leave one fork and one knife," Spencer said because he knew I was about to snap on her. Then, he turned to me and said, "Sweetheart, I'm going to see some friends on the other side of the club, so enjoy your meal, and I will be back shortly."

I felt my cell phone vibrating and "Jody" showed up across the screen. It was Eric. I excitedly answered and put my hand over my mouth to make sure that no one heard me.

"Hello," I said with the biggest smile ever.

"Hey, baby, what are you doing?"

The thought of him calling me "baby" made my knees weak.

"I am out with Spencer."

"I know you are, baby. I just wanted to hear your voice. I want to see you later on."

There was something about his voice, and I could just imagine his dimples on the other end of the phone.

"My uncle trusts you, so you should be able to tell him that you are hanging out with your friends or something."

I did want to hang out with people my age, but the problem was I didn't have any friends. I, sometimes, got tired of listening to Spencer's conversations about golf and sports. I had to act like I was interested by shaking my head like I knew what the fuck a putt was.

"I heard about that new Maybach that my uncle got you. I want to take it for a spin."

"Boy, are you crazy? Your uncle will kill us both."

"We'll figure it out. Just try and get away from him. I will call you back to tell you where to meet me," he said before hanging up.

"Who were you talking to, my dear?" Spencer said as he snuck up on me.

"Oh, that was my friend Tunique. She's going through a breakup, and she needs a shoulder to lean on. I want to go spend a few days with her."

I don't know how in the hell that lie had rolled off my tongue so quick, but it did.

"Sure. No problem. Why don't you get her back on the phone and invite her here to have some fun?"

"She's not a club-going type of person," I said as I put my phone in my purse and thought, *He actually believes me and trusts me after all.*

9
Eric

I didn't know what Eric thought he was doing, but I was going to find out. When we got back to the mansion, I went to the twins' rooms. They both were sound asleep, so I kissed them on their cheeks. My dream was to have a big house with a circle driveway for my twins and me. I didn't want to share it with an old-ass man and a maid, but a girl's got to do what a girl's got to do.

On the way back down the hall, I made a stop at the kitchen and noticed that the back door was open. Just as I was about to close and lock it, Rita came flying through the door.

"What are you doing out there this time of night?" I asked.

"I was looking at the stars," she said as she locked the door. "Your twins are so fun to be with. They gave me a run for my money today. Shelton is so fast. He needs to be a track star."

The look on her face didn't look like she had been looking at any stars. I walked over to the sink and looked out the window and noticed that there was a shed back there that had the words KEEP OUT all over it.

"What's that house back there for?" I asked.

"Oh, that's an old shed where Spencer keeps all of his tools," she nervously said before coming over to close the plantation blinds.

There is something else in there, I thought. *Tools, my ass. Her body language tells me different.* I decided to let that go for the time being. Spencer walked in. He came and stood behind me.

"Sweetie, I am going to miss you," he said.

"I'm only going to be gone for a couple of days," I said as I turned around and hugged his neck.

Rita walked out without saying anything.

"I think I'll just chill out around here with the twins and Rita and catch up on a few things."

"I'll be back before you know it."

I went to the closet to grab a few clothes. I neatly folded my dresses and put them in my Louis Vuitton Monogram Excursion set along with my heels. I couldn't find my makeup bag, so I wandered to Spencer's side of the room. I looked in his closet, and I saw a black briefcase in the middle of the floor. I decided to be nosy and open it up. I found several newspaper clippings that read *"Suspected Kingpin Cleared in Wife's Disappearance"*. I quickly closed it, forgetting all about my makeup bag. *I won't be his next victim. That's for sure*, I thought.

When I walked out the door, I saw Spencer sitting in the great room, looking at the shed on the television screen. That further let me know that something more was back in the shed besides tools. I didn't know what to say on my way out, so I said, "I love you, Spencer. Call you later."

"Love you, too," he said, continuing to look at the screen as I walked out of the door. As soon as I got in the car, I called Eric.

"What's the plan?" I asked as I put on my seatbelt.

He told me where to meet him. I rode off, feeling like I was one of those chicks in the music videos, except my Maybach was not a rental.

When I got to the hotel room, I noticed that Eric didn't have on anything but a pair of boxers. I looked him up and down, and, instantly, I wanted to run into his arms. *I can't resist this boy,* I thought. *Not even if I tried to.*

"I see you got out after all," he said as he grabbed my luggage.

He started kissing me, and I didn't hold back. I tried to put my whole tongue in his mouth. The smell of the Hennessey on his breath and the cologne on his neck made me want to just eat him alive. *He is a piece of work,* I thought.

"Eric, are you sure we can get away with this?"

"We already have," he said as he continued to kiss me.

I knew I was dead-ass wrong, but I didn't care. Spencer hadn't tried to fuck me yet, so what was a girl to do?

I took off my clothes, and we both laid in the king sized bed, looking up at the ceiling.

"Eric, what do you want me to do? I can't keep doing this."

"Yes, you can. Girl, I feel that I am in love with you."

"In love with me?"

"Yes, I am in love with you. I think I would be a better man for you than my uncle."

"Boy, please! You are seventeen, and you're going to be a professional basketball player. You're going to go to college and meet a nice girl."

"I already met a nice girl. I like older women."

"Fool, I'm only three years older than you!"

"That don't matter. You're still the girl I want to be with."

"Don't kid yourself."

I knew I was kidding myself because I didn't want him to be fucking anyone but me.

"What is that supposed to mean?" he asked, looking into my eyes with a serious look.

"It means that I am marrying your uncle, and we can't be a couple."

"Well, you can come see me when I go to college."

"That can be arranged," I said as I laid on top of him.

His eyes had me mesmerized.

"So, what did you tell my uncle for you to get away?"

"I told him that I was going to be a shoulder for a friend."

"Good one," he said as he started kissing me again. "I want to hit that pussy from the back."

I got up and bent over, and he slid his dick into my wet pussy. My body was tingling. He really knew how to work his big-ass dick.

"Throw it back, baby! Throw it back," he repeated.

He was slapping me on my ass as I threw it back. I loved it when he talked to me while we were having sex.

"I'm 'bout to cum, baby! I'm 'bout to fill your good, wet pussy up! Are you ready for me to fill it up?"

"Yes, Eric! Yes, Eric!"

"I love you, baby! I really do," he said, trying to hold back.

"I love you, too! Fuck me harder! Fuck me harder!"

I felt the warmth of his sperm as he let loose inside my wet pussy. Then, he laid flat on his back on the other side of the bed. I laid on his chest, thinking, *What the hell have I got myself into?*

10
Hanging Out with Eric

Eric and I got up and ordered room service. We were in a suite in downtown Atlanta. Every time I felt his eyes watching me, I'd think, *How long can we do this?,* but, like he said, the damage had already been done.

Eric poured himself a shot of Hennessey.

"Why are you drinking so early?"

"Because I am about to be a rich motherfucker who is about to go to the NBA."

"You haven't been accepted yet, so don't count your eggs before they hatch."

"Yeah. You're right because, if I don't make it, you can take care of me."

I almost choked on my orange juice.

"You are not making any sense to me right now. What do you mean 'I can take care of you'?"

"I'm just saying. If I don't make it to the pros, you'll be my backbone just like my uncle is your backbone."

I didn't know what to think. I wasn't caught in a love triangle because I didn't love Spencer at all. Eric had said that he loved me, and I thought I loved him, too. I sure as hell didn't love Spencer. That was for sure.

"I have our night planned out. We're going to go to a club a few blocks from here," Eric informed me.

"Boy, I can't be seen with you at a club, especially not in public. Spencer has eyes all over the world," I said as I got up and closed the blinds.

"Quit worrying so much, will you? Just trust me on this. Let's just have fun this weekend."

"Okay, Eric. Whatever you say."

Eric put on a black, red, and gray Jordan sweat suit with the Jordans to match. *He will fit right into the league,* I thought.

Eric insisted on driving my car. I knew that I was in over my head already. If he drove my car, and someone saw us together, how would I explain that to Spencer if that news got back to him? I thought about that and realized that would have to be a bridge I would have to cross when I got to it.

"Slow down," I said as I looked around, eyeing my surroundings as we left. "Why are you driving so fast?"

It was a good thing that there were no police in sight.

"Girl, you got a race car, and you have to put the pedal to the medal."

He was running through red lights and speeding down the main streets like we were unstoppable!

"What are we doing here?" I asked as we pulled up to his mansion. "Where is your mother? She can't see us together. What about the security cameras?"

I had a million questions going through my mind.

"Girl, don't worry. My mother isn't here, and I can edit the security cameras. No one will see you on them."

When we got to his room, he popped open a CD and put it in the DVD player.

"What is this? Some type of joke?" I asked as I looked at us on the screen. "What is this shit, Eric?"

I walked towards the television. "You recorded us having sex? Why did you do this?"

"Calm down," he said as he ejected the disc. "This is my insurance, and this will not get back to my uncle if you do everything that I tell you. My uncle is filthy rich, and I have been trying to be like him for years."

"You're going to the NBA, dummy!"

"That's all a bunch of bullshit that I told them, so they could stay off of my ass. I was going at first, but I started gambling and getting into different shit, and they cut me from the team. Hell! They denied me from going to college. It all started when me and my boy Cameron went down to take a tour of the college. I swear I had my head on straight. I really wanted to play ball. I got game, too! We went the opposite way of the college and hooked up with one of Cameron's cousins. We went to a gambling spot that got busted by the police. It was a small town, and news traveled fast. It had got back to the school, and that was the end of my career. I didn't tell anyone."

"Well, why are you using me?"

"Because you are an easy target. You gave the pussy up so quick. I told you all that shit, so you'd fall for me."

I wanted to jump up and choke him. I heard him when he said that he had filled my head up with a bunch of bullshit, but I felt different. I felt that he had some type of love for me because he had looked directly into my eyes when we made love, if that was what he called it. *The nerve of this young bastard.* I had to think of a plan quick and get him out of my life for good.

" Why don't you just ask Spencer for money? He loves you. He'll take care of you."

"He will be very disappointed in me if he finds out that I didn't go to school. I actually thought about blackmailing him because I remember the night Auntie Jo Ann went missing. I was about seven years old, and I remember them having a big fight. I was at his mansion at the time, and I watched from the top of the stairs as he hit her repeatedly in her face and head. He kept saying over and over, 'You thought you could cheat on me and get away with it?' She wasn't the one cheating; he was.

She had a razor, and she slashed at his dick, and I think she cut it off. By the way, has my uncle fucked you yet?"

I couldn't begin to speak. I was still trying to register all that he just said had taken place when he was seven years old.

"I know a lot of things about him that no one else knows."

"Please tell me! I have to go get my twins out of that house!"

"No, you won't. You will do as I tell you, or you and your twins will be missing like Auntie Jo Ann! Now, you're going to go back home and act like everything is cool, and I will let you know what I want you to do. You will marry him, and you will have access to the safe that he has in his wine cellar. He has millions of dollars in there. He has been an untouchable kingpin. No one can touch him in any kind of way. And you will give me five thousand dollars per month, and you will get me a penthouse downtown, and you will let me drive your Maybach whenever I want to."

"Are you fucking serious?"

"Serious as a heart attack," he said as he lifted up the disc. "Now, I want you to get up, put on some of that fly shit, and let's go to the club."

"Is Spencer a drug dealer?"

"You mean to tell me you don't know that you are about to marry one of the wealthiest crime lords around?"

"What the hell have I got myself into?"

"You got yourself into some quicksand, and you're in it up to your neck. Everyone will live happily ever after if you just do what I say."

My first response was to get up and run, but if I had done that he would have shown Spencer the DVD of us, and my twins and I would have been dead!

11
The Three Amigos

There had been a change of plans, and we didn't go to the club after all. I wanted to go to Spencer's mansion and get my kids and leave town, but where could I go?

Eric took me back to the hotel, and he left. He told me that he was going to drive to West Georgia to see one of his girlfriends. I was pissed off! I was a wingless fly caught in Eric's web. There was nothing I could do. He wanted me to give him five thousand a month and let him drive my car whenever he felt like it. At that time, I really needed God to appear and just take my twins and me away. I decided to play Eric's game. I could get down and dirty, too. I would just tell Spencer that Eric had seduced me and given me a date rape drug. *That's it! He seemed to believe anything I said, anyway.*

As I was about to dial Spencer's number, I thought about what I was saying on the disc. How could I explain the words that were coming out of my mouth? I had told Eric, in the midst of us fucking, that I loved his young, hard dick. I had said a lot more stuff to him. I even said that I wanted to marry him instead of Spencer. The dick could be so powerful, at times.

I couldn't believe Eric had recorded us.

"Shit!" I screamed real loud as I laid across the king sized bed.

"Think, Tameka, think!" I said as I hit myself on the forehead.

This wasn't funny anymore. I never thought it was. I was just trying to get away with sleeping with my man's nephew, but it had backfired.

I heard the door open. It was Eric.

"I thought you was going to see your little girlfriend," I said sarcastically. "Eric, why are you doing this to me? I thought you really had feelings for me? Don't I suck your dick good?"

I walked over to him and rubbed on his dick.

"There has been a change of plans. My uncle called me, and he wants me to go with him to pick out a tuxedo for the wedding."

"But he hasn't even told me a date, yet?"

"He told me, and it's soon. The sooner, the better," he said as he slouched down on the bed.

"Look, Eric. Can we talk about this?"

"There's nothing to talk about! I'm not going to the NBA, so you're going to marry my uncle, and we'll all be happy!"

"Can you change your tone with me then? Do you hate me, or is this just business?"

"It's business and personal," he said as he took off his t-shirt. "Now, get over here and give me some of that pussy."

"You got to be out of your mind? How the hell are you going to blackmail me and still fuck me?"

"Easy," he said as he grabbed me and threw me on the bed.

His eyes went from green to blue. His dimples and his sexy, wet lips turned me on. I was crazy to bend over and let him fuck me, but it was too late. My feelings were involved. Not only was I attracted to him, but it was almost like I needed his sex. I loved it when he talked to me. I loved it when he looked me in my eyes with his two-toned colored eyes and grabbed my neck. He was my fantasy man. Spencer wasn't fucking me, and I didn't want to fuck him, anyway. If Twinkie was alive and she had to go through this shit that I was going through with Eric, I bet she would have cut off Eric's dick and fed it to him. I had no choice but to do as I was told, and that was to get on my knees and assume the position. He slid his dick in me, and I was soaking wet in an instant. I moaned, and I arched my back and used my muscles in my pussy to grip his dick.

He said, "Baby, what are you doing? How did you do that?"

"Do what?" I said as I gripped his dick again.

In my mind, I wanted to have him hooked on my sex, too.

"Stop that," he said as he slapped me on my ass.

"Stop what?" I said as I continued to grip his hard dick.

"I see now you want me to whoop you."

He pulled my hair and slapped me on my ass, saying, "This is what you need. You need a real man to whoop this pussy."

I was throwing it back, and I felt him just let his body go.

"Turn over, baby," he whispered as he turned me over on my back.

My pussy was so wet. I had already busted so many nuts just by him talking to me...just by the Hennessey on his breath...just by the Sean John cologne on his body. He got on top of me, and he grabbed my face and kissed me as he eased his hard dick in me. He had to be the son of the devil, but I didn't see any horns on the top of his head.

"Throw it back, baby! Yeah! Just like that!"

"Eric, how can you do this to me?"

"We'll be together in the end," he said as he pumped harder.

I moaned and asked, "How are we going to be together, Eric? How?"

"You'll see, baby. I have a plan. Just go along with it."

I loved it when he called me "baby". It just did something to me. I didn't care what happened. I just wanted him to stay in my pussy all day. He finally released his thick, warm sperm in me, and I felt it as his dick jerked as it flowed out. I got up to take a shower.

While I was in the shower, I couldn't stop thinking about what he said. *How were we going to be together in the end? Is he going to kill Spencer? What kind of plan does he have?* All sorts of questions were going through my head. I was in a deadly game of cat and mouse. I couldn't be the mouse that always got caught in the mouse trap. I definitely had to be the cat that walked away with nine lives.

Eric came into the bathroom and sat on the toilet while I was in the shower.

"Hurry up and put on some clothes. I just talked to my uncle, and I told him that we were together."

"What!" I said as I snatched the shower curtain back.

"Calm down! I told him I saw you, and you gave me a ride."

My heart was racing, and it felt like it was in my throat. He stood in front of the shower with a towel as I got out. I thought that the gesture was so nice of him. I felt deep down inside that he did have love for me, too. He dried me off from my shoulders to my breasts and all the way down to the bottom of my feet. I grabbed his face and looked down at him as he was drying me off and said, "I know you got some feelings for me in that ice-cold heart of yours."

"You're right. I do, but, right now, we have to get this money from my uncle, so we can live happily ever after with the twins."

It all sounded too good to be true, but, when you got money, anything is possible.

"We're going to go live somewhere far away," he said as he drifted off into space.

I pulled my hair back in a ponytail and slid on a short set.

"Let's go," he said as he grabbed my keys.

"Wait a minute. You can't drive us to Spencer's," I said as I tried to get the keys from him.

I looked real foolish, jumping up and down, trying to take the keys from that six-foot boy.

"Eric, we have to be logical and reasonable," I said, being dead serious. "What would we look like pulling up at Spencer's with you driving?"

"I'll just tell him I was taking it for a test drive."

I was already in deep shit. It couldn't get any deeper than this. I sat in my Maybach and put in my Rick Ross CD.

"Yeah. This is my jam," he said before speeding off.

When we arrived at Spencer's, he and Evelyn were talking. They were sitting at the top of the terrace.

"Just act normal," Eric said through his teeth as he spoke to Spencer. "What's up, uncle? I love that car. You must really love her."

"Yes, I love her, and, maybe when you're older, you'll find a woman just like her."

"You better take good care of my brother," Evelyn said, looking me up and down with an attitude. "He's all I've got left."

Spencer walked over and hugged me.

"I missed you," he said as he kissed me on my neck.

"I missed you, too, sweetheart. Where are the twins?" I said as I looked around.

"They're out with Rita," he replied.

"So, when is the big day?" Evelyn asked.

I looked at Spencer because I wanted to know, too.

"We're going to fly to Italy," Spencer said as he looked over at me.

"Italy! I haven't even been to Columbus, Georgia! Hell! I have never been out of town!"

"Nephew, I want you to tag along with us."

"I'd love to, Unk."

Could this shit get any worse?, I wondered.

"Unk, we're going to have so much fun," Eric said as he looked at me with a wicked look on his face.

"Well, y'all have fun. I'm going to go on a mini-vacation myself," Evelyn said. "I'm going to go to Mexico and get my groove back. I can still drop it like it's hot."

"You go, girl," I said with a fake smile.

I wandered off to the kitchen, telling everyone I was going to fix myself a glass of water, but, I took a shot of vodka, instead.

"Fix me one, too," I heard Eric say.

"Did you tell Spencer anything about us?"

"No, baby. Our secret is safe with me. He don't suspect a thing. He didn't say anything about me driving your four hundred thousand dollar car. You're going to be married to the mob, and there's only one way out, and that is death."

I had a plan of my own, and it would come into play as soon as Spencer and I got married, but, first, I had go visit my brother in the county jail.

12
Brotherly Love

When I got to the Fulton County Jail, everyone that worked there was so damn rude, including the fucking janitor.

"May I help you?" one woman asked as she looked at the clipboard she was holding.

"Uh. Yes, ma'am. I need to see my brother George. George Simmons."

"George Simmons," she said as she checked the computer. "Ah, ha. Found him, but he's no longer here. He was here for three weeks. Then, he got transported to Cobb County. They have some type of probation hold on him. There is no telling what type of holds he has on him because he did everything from selling drugs to stealing cars."

Twinkie didn't ever get any respect from George. They would always bump heads about something. She never told us who our daddy was, and that was why George was so mad at her because he had always wanted a daddy. As far as I was concerned, we were both trick babies. It didn't matter to me because I was going to make it in this cruel world one way or another. While the officer talked to me, I kept getting more and more irritated because she was the same officer that I had run into numerous times when I was in the streets.

Back then, she'd say, "You better be glad that I am arresting your ass and not calling your loved ones to identify your body."

As I headed to the Cobb County Jail, I reflected on my fucked-up past. When I was in the streets, I didn't care if I died or not because I didn't have anyone. I was just a free spirit, and

I felt, at times, that my breath was just a waste. The only person I did have was George, and he made it fun when he came up off a lick. I was living in Decatur, and that was when I met my pimp. Money Toney was his name, and all the bitches in the streets reported to him, old and young. I lived here and there, and I had a friend named Keisha who often whored with me.

One night, we walked to the gas station, and that was when we first saw Money Toney. He was sitting in a white, short dog Cadillac. The rims on his car definitely caught my attention. I didn't know he was a pimp until he said, "I got a way that you fine-ass, young girls can make plenty of money."

Keisha was down for whatever, and so was I, but I didn't know that I had to suck different dicks and get fucked by men of all ages. The money was good, but we couldn't keep it. We had to work the streets all day and all night and turn our money over to him. He put us up in different hotels. We never really had a decent place to stay. He'd always say, "I keep the money because that's what pimps do."

Money Toney had a rival pimp, and his name was Lowe. Keisha left us to go work for him. I didn't care who pimped me. I was looking for love in all the wrong places. I remember when I hooked up with a married trick named Mike. I didn't make him put on a rubber when I sucked his dick or fucked him. I was young and dumb, and I didn't know that all diseases aren't visible. I didn't mind sucking his dick because it was all a part of the business. I swallowed his sperm, but it wasn't healthy sperm at all.

Three days later, I had a bad infection in my throat. Money Toney didn't say anything but, "I told your stupid ass to strap up." He didn't show me any love, and I had to continue on until, one day, my body almost shut down. I was fucked up. I couldn't speak because my throat was swollen. I had a fever of 106 degrees Fahrenheit. Finally, he dropped me off at Grady's teen clinic. I had gonorrhea in my throat, ears, and my nose. The doctor told me that, if I had waited any longer, it could have spread to my eyes, and I could have been blind. I was on all types of antibiotics and penicillin, but those were the good old days when I made plenty of money for Money Toney.

When I arrived at the Cobb County Jail, I knew time wasn't on my side. I had to meet Spencer and Eric back at the mansion. I didn't know what Spencer had in store for me, but he never did say when we were getting married. All eyes were on me as I stepped out of my Maybach. I stepped out with my hater blockers on, and they must have thought I was Lil Kim or somebody.

"Let me get that door for you," one officer said as I walked in without saying shit to him.

I hated all cops. They used to fuck with me in the streets for no reason. Now that I looked like a celebrity, they didn't know how to act. When I got to the window, a female officer greeted me. She looked like a dyke. I thought she was a man until I saw her breasts poking out like Dolly Parton's as I got closer. Her hair was cut short, and she wasn't very tall.

"May I help you?" she said as I approached the window.

"Yes, ma'am. I am trying to bond my brother George Simmons out of jail."

"I remember him," she said as she looked at the computer. "There is a hold on him, so he can't be bonded out right now. His probationer officer is on vacation, so it looks like he'll be sitting for a while."

"What kind of hold? I have money."

"I'm afraid money can't get him out this time."

"Okay. Well, can I, at least, see him?"

I took my shades off, so she could see my eyes.

"Well, visiting hours are over."

I threw three crisp one hundred dollar bills down on the counter in front of her. Money talks, and bullshit walks.

"Not a problem," she said as she led the way through the smelly-ass jail.

Cops are good for something after all, I thought as we walked down the corridor.

13
Three-Time Loser

"Man, sis, they got me in here under a warrant," George said as he sat down.

"It's going to be okay. I'm going to get you the best lawyers that money can buy. Hang on a second," I said as I went to ask the officer if she could take the handcuffs and shackles off of him. "Damn, I just gave you three hundred dollars. Can I, at least, hug my brother?"

"You're pushing it," she said.

"No, bitch! You're pushing it," I snapped back. Then, I turned to my brother and said, "I met an old-ass kingpin named Spencer, and we're getting married soon. He is sweet as pie. He don't question my actions. Plus, I'm fucking his nephew who is blackmailing me right now."

"Hold up! Back up!" George said, giving a sigh of relief once his handcuffs were removed.

"What do you mean 'he's blackmailing you'?"

"I have it under control, George. We're in love, and we're basically using Spencer, and, in the end, we're going to be together."

"So, I can't rob the nigga?" George asked with a serious look on his face.

"No, he's not that type of cat. If I'm straight, then you're straight. Now, tell me what happened? Did Miss Gladys have anything to do with this shit?"

George had rented a trap apartment in the same projects where Bernard and I lived. He sold drugs out of it and fucked different girls in it.

"No, it was that bitch Keisha."

"Wait a minute. Are you talking about my homegirl Keisha?"

"Yes. Your homegirl Keisha," he repeated. "She came to the spot to buy a quarter pound of weed, and, when I went to the back to get the scale, she stole all my weed and crack. I know she did it because, when I came back to the front, she was gone, and she left the door wide open!"

"What!" I said in disbelief.

"But I am going to get that bitch, though."

"No, you're not. I am going to get that bitch for you," I said as I pounded my fist in my hand. "The nerve of that bitch... and I was going to pick her up and get her out of that ghetto life. It's been a while since I've seen her, but we were good friends. I guess all that friend shit is thrown out of the window if you're not blood. George, you just have to stay calm, and I am going to get you out of here."

"Well, sis, I'm going to tell you like this. I am a three-time felon, and these crackers are already trying to roast a nigga. They got me on some old shit that happened back in the day. I robbed three Mexicans, and I killed they ass right where they stood," George said as he sat back in the chair and fired up a cigarette. "The only thing that got me fucked up was the security camera. It caught a glimpse of my tattoos. And you know I can't go unnoticed with all these tattoos over my body. Those Mexicans were sweet, too. I had to do what I had to do. I wouldn't be a gangster if I'd let that opportunity walk."

My heart sunk in my stomach. I felt like I had to throw up.

"George, did you actually kill those people?" I calmly asked.

"Look. Twinkie didn't do a lot of shit, but she didn't raise no punk-ass man. She raised me for a part of my life, and, for the rest of it, I was raised by the streets."

"Well, did you pray before you killed them? Do gangsters pray?" I asked again with tears rolling down my face.

"Sis, look. I'm going to tell you just like this. They knew that there was a chance they'd get killed in the dope game. They knew there was a possibility that they might not see their families again. I see this shit for what it is. I'm going to die in the streets or behind these bars. It's just that simple. The life I live is fast. If I live by the sword, I will most certainly die by the sword. I know there is a God, and I will have to answer to Him for all the shit I've done, so I will have no problem killing that cat you fucking with if you give me the okay."

"No," I said quickly. "He has the twins' and my best interest at heart. We live in a big mansion, and he bought me a Maybach."

"Well, since you like the nigga, I'll let the nigga breathe."

I knew right then and there that my brother didn't give a fuck about anything. He didn't care about the next man's life or his own life, for that matter.

"I will keep in touch. You just sit tight," I said.

"Where the fuck am I going to go? These crackers watch a nigga's every move."

"I know, George. I am going to do all I can to get you out. I love you so much," I said as I stood up to hug him.

"I love you, too, sis. Take care of the twins, and don't worry about me. I am a gangster until I die."

That was what I was afraid of.

14

Insurance is Better than Playing the Lottery

I was ready to marry Spencer, so my own plan could go into play. I wouldn't mind spending the rest of my life with Eric, but I knew he couldn't be a father figure to my twins because he was a teenager, but who needed a daddy when you were filthy rich? I had forgotten all about Bernard's sorry-ass. I hoped he was somebody's bitch in jail. He was worthless, anyway. As long as Spencer loved me and gave me my space and I could fuck Eric whenever I wanted, I was cool. When I arrived back at Spencer's, I mentioned to him about getting George out of jail, but I didn't know if that was such a good idea, considering George would kill anybody for money. Spencer told me that he would try to get with his connections downtown.

"Are you sure you're ready to be Mrs. Spencer Davis?" Spencer asked as he came closer.

"I sure am," I said without a doubt. "Why wouldn't I be?"

I watched Eric out the corner of my eye. I thought that he had gone home. *Why was he still here?*

"Well, first, I want you to sign this fifty million dollar life insurance policy."

My heart was screaming on the inside, as I calmly said, "Fifty million dollars. What is this for?"

"This covers only accidental death."

Now, I thought for sure that I wouldn't get out of the marriage alive.

"Eric is my witness, and he is the second beneficiary on here in case something happens to you."

Now, I knew that this was do or die with Eric for real. Eric walked over and signed under my name.

"Damn, Unk! You plan on checking out anytime soon?" Eric asked as he signed his name.

"Nephew, you can never be too careful. In this life, one day, you're here, and the next day, you're gone."

I looked at Eric, and I knew that it was do or die with Spencer, also.

"So, we'll be one big, happy family," I said sarcastically as I saw the evil in Eric's eyes.

Spencer had let it be known we were getting married in Italy, and everyone was coming, including Rita, the twins, Evelyn, and Eric.

I was so glad to see my twins when Rita walked in with them.

"Mommy," they said as they both ran and hugged me.

It seemed like it had been ages since I had seen them. Shelton was looking more like Bernard, and Sherita was looking more like me. They had everything that children could possibly want. Rita kept them busy while I went on my various rendezvous. I loved my twins, but, when I looked into their eyes, all I could think about was what I had gotten us into. *How will I get us out of this one?*, I wondered. The twins and I went upstairs, leaving Spencer and Eric downstairs.

"Guess what, twins?" I said as I closed the door. "I have some good news. Spencer and I are getting married, and you guys will never have to work a day in your lives."

The twins were getting older, and they knew about working hard. I had always told them, if I ever caught a break in life, they would be straight. Well, Spencer was that break.

"Knock! Knock!"

I heard a voice as I sat in my room. I turned and saw that it was Evelyn's nosy ass. I didn't like her.

"So, do you have the bubble gut?" she asked as she stared at my twins.

"No, I don't," I replied.

"Where is the father of your kids?"

"In jail, where he belongs," I snapped.

"Well, I know you only want money from my brother. He's too blind to see it, but I know you're nothing but a gold digger. Look at the way you dress. You wear dresses that are skin tight, and you wear shorts that are so short that the crack of your black ass shows. I know you couldn't possibly love him. You look familiar. What's your mother's name?"

I knew Evelyn wasn't feeling me, but I didn't care. I was marrying her brother, and I was fucking her son. She was right, but I couldn't let her know.

"What makes you ask that?" I asked like I gave a damn.

I didn't care what she thought because, once I married Spencer, I could care less what she thought about me.

"You are wrong," I said with a straight face. "I do love Spencer, and I am not using him."

"You look very familiar," she said again as she sat on an ottoman.

"Where are you from? Are you from Georgia or Africa?"

I was dark-skinned, but why would this bitch think that I was from Africa?

"Don't worry about where she's from," Spencer said as he entered the room. "We leave our pasts in the past. Now, Evelyn, Rita needs you to help her in the shed."

Evelyn hurried away without saying another word.

"What's in the shed?" I asked.

"Oh, nothing much. Rita's just out there, rearranging the tools and things."

Every time I asked him about that shed, he'd quickly make up a lie about it or change the subject. I wasn't a fool, and neither was I stupid. I was going in that shed one way or another.

"Sweetheart, my life has become so complete with you," he said as he patted Shelton on the head.

"Come on, baby. Let's make love," he whispered in my ear.

15
Sexual Relations – Ugh!

This would actually be the first time that Spencer and I officially had sex. He'd always slobber on my pussy, and I'd act interested and pretend to cum, but I was not ready for this.

When I laid on the bed, he pulled his clothes off, and I was speechless. He didn't have a dick or even a baby dick. Hell! He didn't even have balls!

"What the fuck? Oops! I didn't mean to blurt that out, but where's your dick? How are we going to have sex when you don't have no dick?"

"Don't worry," he said as he pulled out a huge strap-on from under the bed.

"And what's that bag on you? Is that a shit bag? You better not get any of that shit on me? What is that, Spencer? You should have warned me first. You just can't drop your boxers and shock the shit out of me."

There was a little voice in my head, trying to tell me to shut the fuck up, but it was too late. I was in a state of shock. I walked over to the mini bar and drunk out of the Hennessey bottle.

"Sweetheart, I know this is a lot to deal with, but I know that you have love for me, and this is how I wanted to show you. It's been months, and we haven't been together. I should have told you sooner, but the truth is I have cancer, and my doctor had to operate immediately upon finding out."

"How the hell did you get cancer in the dick?"

"It's a long story that I do not care to talk about right now," he said as he looked at the huge vibrator. "I can make you feel better with this, though. Here. Feel it."

He walked over to me. I turned up the bottle again as I felt the vibrator.

"It's warm," I said as I grabbed it out of his hand.

"It's a special one that I had made just for you."

"You make sure that bag with that piss and shit doesn't leak out on me?"

"I will detach it," he said as he took it loose and put about four inches of gauze on it. Then, he secured it with a band aid. The Hennessey wasn't working quick enough on my brain. I had to be under the influence to get fucked by a dickless man. Even though Spencer was very handsome, knowing he didn't have a dick made it very difficult to get in the mood. It was a real mind-blower.

"How come you can't go buy a dick?" I asked jokingly as he laid me on my back.

For fifty million dollars, I would have to get used to getting fucked by a plastic dick. I was thinking, *God, please let this fuck go by quick.*

"Am I hurting you?" he asked as he eased the warm vibrator into of me.

"No, you're good," I said, wanting him to hurry up.

I laid there and moaned and pretended like I was enjoying it, but I was sick to my stomach. I wished he had hidden the shit bag. It was to the right of me on his night stand. When he was done, I just laid in the bed, wrapped in the sheets. I wondered how long I would have to pretend to like this. That voice inside my head said I had fifty millions reasons.

16
A Night on the Town

The next morning, when I woke up, I found a note that Spencer had left. It said that he had to go out of town on business. *Good*, I thought because for a minute I dreamed I had gotten fucked by a fake dick. Then, I looked on the floor, and I realized that I wasn't dreaming. It was real. Spencer had left it on the floor. How weird was that? I washed it off and put it back in the closet with the rest of his plastic dicks.

I went to the kitchen to fix a cup of coffee. I looked at the shed through the kitchen window. *This is my chance to go to see what or who is in the shed*, I thought because, if Spencer's wife was in there, I could free her. Just as I was about to open the back door, I heard Evelyn's voice, saying, "So, are you ready to pick up where we left off in our conversation?"

"No," I answered as I left her standing there with a blank look on her face.

I took a shower and put on a Nike sweat suit. I went to the projects to let everyone over there know that I was looking for Keisha. I was going to kick her ass for stealing from my brother. I couldn't believe she would do that after all the free weed I used to give her. There was no sign of her. No one knew where she was.

After I left the projects, I stopped and grabbed a few dresses from Bianca at Phipps Plaza. Thanks to me, she received a big commission. Then, I headed downtown. I checked into a room at the Four Seasons and wasted time there until I decided to go to the club. I had always wanted to go to a club and just toss the valet the keys to park my car. On TV, that had looked so cool to me. I was looking good, and I stepped out looking like I was ready to mingle. I pulled up at Studio 72. It must have been college night or something because there were students everywhere. I pulled up in my black and red Maybach. I did what I saw on TV, and that was throw my keys to the valet. Everyone looked at me like I was famous. I saw that the line was very long, but I didn't stand in a line. I paid fifty dollars and went to the bar. The club had so many amenities to offer. It was designed with such elegance. The neon lights throughout were a plus.

"What can I get for you?" the waiter asked.

"A Colt 45," I replied.

"What is a Colt 45? I've never heard of it," he said as he looked over the drink menu.

"It's a beer! You know the one that Billy Dee Williams drinks?"

"Who's Billy Dee Williams?"

"You've got to be kidding me. You mean to tell me you don't know who Billy Dee is."

I was looking around to see if I could spot a poster with Billy Dee on it advertising Colt 45, but those could only be found in the hood.

"Sorry, ma'am. We only have imported beer."

"I'll take a bucket of Corona with Rosie's Lime."

While I sat at the bar, I watched the people dance on the dance floor. They were looking good, grinding on each other. They reminded me of the girls that danced freaky in the rap videos. After about three or four beers, I headed to the dance floor. I was dancing and moving my hips to R. Kelly's "Bump and Grind". I was rolling my hips and pulling on my hair like I was an exotic dancer. I felt all eyes on me. I loved being the center of attention at the right time. And in there, definitely, was the right time. Then, I felt someone come up on me to dance with me from behind. It was Eric. I should have known it was him because I didn't know anyone else in there.

"What's up, baby?" he asked as he grabbed me by my waist and kept on dancing.

"Are you following me?" I asked.

"Of course not. This is the spot I come to when I want to get away. Plus, it's college night."

"How did your young ass get in here?"

"When you got money, nothing else matters. Besides, aren't you glad to see me?" he said as he slapped me on my ass.

"Yes, I am glad to see you," I said as I kissed him on his neck.

"Come on over here with me to the VIP area."

When we got to the VIP area, I noticed that there were more glasses and bottles. This let me know that Eric wasn't alone. *Who could he be here with?* I thought.

"I see you like Hennessey," I said as I poured myself a shot.

"You like it, too," he said as he came closer.

He smelled so good. I could just eat him up. I was really falling for this boy. I knew that my emotions were getting the best of me, but I didn't care.

"Eric, since Spencer has you on the policy, can you please destroy the disc of us?"

"No, no, no. I can't do that. I am not going to the league, remember? I need you to get the five grand, and I need you to get me a loft."

"Eric, you have my heart. You do not have to blackmail me."

"I will do what I feel is necessary to do, so please stop asking me."

He kissed me, and I began to melt. I forgot all about the blackmail.

"Damn! Who is this?" his friend asked as he sat down on the sofa next to us.

"Rodney, this is my girlfriend Tameka, and this fool is my best friend in the whole wide world. His name is Rodney."

"Damn, she is fine," I heard a female say as she joined us.

"And this chickenhead is my bisexual girlfriend Jade," Rodney said.

"This is my man. We have been together since the third grade," Jade said.

Jade was pretty and very drunk.

"We had one threesome together, and he has been crazy about me ever since. He picks 'em, and I lick 'em," she said as she licked her lips at me.

"Well, you can't have her," Eric said as he grabbed my hand.

"You don't know what she can have," I said as I snatched my hand away from him and walked over and kissed her.

Eric and Rodney turned into shocked, horny dogs. I shocked myself. The Hennessey was kicking in, and the more I looked at Eric, the more I wanted to go back to my room and fuck. I was turned on by her light complexion and thick thighs. She looked like Trina. Her hair was short and curly. She had on a white collar shirt, black suspenders, and a plaid skirt. I had never been with a girl before, but she was so direct. She kind of reminded me of myself, and she was so head strong. She could definitely be on my team. She didn't hold back. She grabbed me, and we stood up and danced right there in VIP. We were grabbing each other's breasts and slipping each other's hands under each others' skirts. The boys couldn't handle it. They both got up, and Eric danced behind me, and Rodney danced behind her.

"Damn, baby. You got my dick hard," Eric whispered in my ear.

I rubbed my ass against his gray, freshly starched, crisp Levi's, and, sure enough, his dick was as hard as a rock.

"I have a room downtown, baby. Do you want us to go finish what we started there?"

"Hell, yeah! Let's go!"

We grabbed our things and went to the room I had downtown.

17

An Awesome Foursome

Eric and I arrived at my suite at the Four Seasons first. Rodney and Jade were right behind us. They had rode in her car.

"Damn, baby. I didn't know you got down like that," Eric said as he took off his shirt.

"There's a lot of shit you don't know about me," I said as I opened the door for our company.

"There you are," Jade said as her drunk behind fell in my arms.

"You're a great kisser," I told her.

She reeked of alcohol.

"Well, I am a good pussy eater, too," she said as she slipped her finger under my dress.

"You're all she talked about on our ride over here," Rodney said.

"Well, don't just stand there. Lay down on this big, comfy bed," Jade told me.

Eric and Rodney stood there, speechless.

"Oh, you smell so good," she said as she took my panties off with her mouth. "I like the way you have your pussy shaved."

She began to kiss my pussy. She kissed from my inner thighs all the way to my ankles.

I looked up and saw Eric with his dick in his hand. I signaled for him to bring that dick to me. Eric put his dick in my mouth, while Jade was eating my pussy, and Rodney was fucking her from the back. Everyone was being satisfied.

"Your pussy tastes just how you look— good," she said as she continued to slurp on my wet pussy.

She was eating my pussy good. She was doing it at the right degree. When she was on the clit, she stayed on it. She didn't stray away from it like most men did.

While she was eating me, I was enjoying sucking Eric's dick. That boy really had a hold of me. Eric was moaning because I was sucking his dick good, and Jade was moaning because Rodney was fucking her hard from the back. I had to have mind control because I was about to cum on several different occasions. I didn't want to cum in her mouth. I wanted to cum on Eric's dick.

"That's enough," Eric said. "I am ready to fuck my baby."

We got up and went to the other bed. I got a glimpse at Rodney's dick, and it was big, too. Eric and I fucked like wild animals, screaming each others' names and scratching each others' backs. Rodney and Jade were doing moves I hadn't seen anyone do, except maybe porn stars.

"Hey, Eric! Can I fuck your girl? I'll let you fuck mine," Rodney said.

"That's up to her," Eric said as he kissed me.

"Hell, no!" I said.

"Come on," Jade added. "It'll be fun."

"Have you fucked her before?" Rodney asked Eric.

"No. I haven't. That's college shit that they do. I'm not in college, remember?"

"Well, the answer is still no," I said.

"What's the matter? Are you scared that, after I fuck you, you won't want Eric's dick anymore?"

"You're a shit talker," I said as I walked over to where he and Jade were.

"Let me see your dick," I demanded.

He pulled it out of Jade's pussy, and it was soaked with her juices. Her juices were dripping off of his dick and onto the sheets. She was the real meaning of being soaking wet. I looked at Eric. Then, I looked back at Rodney.

"Come on over here on this bed, Eric, and fuck her."

She was laying there, playing in her pussy, rubbing her clit. He was about to dive in her pussy bare dick and all until I said, "Boy, if you don't grab that Magnum off the dresser and strap up."

Then, I looked at Rodney and said, "You better go ahead and strap yours up, too. No glove, no love."

"I don't care what you put on with me, Eric. You can wrap a trash bag around your big-ass dick," Jade said as she continued to play in her pussy.

I watched them both strap up. Then, I looked at Jade, and she was squirming around in the bed like she hadn't been fucked in ages. I watched Eric bend over and slide his dick into her. She screamed his name. I grabbed Rodney and threw him on the bed. Then, I jumped on his dick. The harder I saw Eric fuck Jade, the harder I rode Rodney. Rodney put a firm grip on my ass with both of his hands and moved my ass up and down as I rode him. Eric was looking at me while he was fucking her from the back, and I was looking at him while I was riding Rodney like I was riding a bull. Then, I looked into Rodney's eyes as I was tearing his dick up. He had tears in his eyes. He was rolling his head from side to side on the pillows. It was kind of funny to me because, as freaky as Jade was, I couldn't believe she didn't ride his dick like a maniac. Or she probably didn't know how to clamp her pussy down on his dick like I did. I looked over at Eric, and he had snatched off the Magnum and skeeted his sperm on Jade's ass. It looked so good coming out. I looked down at Rodney just as he came. Our rhythm slowed down. Then, Eric came and got in the bed with me, and

Rodney went and got in the bed with Jade. I laid on Eric's chest and fell asleep like a baby.

18
Back at Spencer's

As time went on, I continued to sleep with Eric, and Spencer didn't have a clue. I had access to the safe, so, each month, I was giving Eric the five grand that he had asked for. I wasn't a mathematician, but I knew that there were billions in cash in that safe. And the more I took, the more it looked like the money grew.

However, I didn't get him a loft like he had asked. Instead, I got myself one downtown, and I let him stay in it. Spencer never questioned me about anything, so I felt that it was okay for Eric to live in my loft. As a matter of fact, Spencer got the loft for me and the twins. I didn't care too much about being in the mansion with Rita at times, so I stayed at my loft when I wanted, and I stayed at Spencer's when I wanted. It was just that simple. I had it made. I could come and go as I pleased. Spencer and I still hadn't gotten married, and, according to his insurance policy, we didn't have to be married in order for me to get the fifty million dollars. It had been a while since we had heard from Rodney and Jade. That foursome was a night I would never forget. George was still locked down. Spencer said that he had used all his power to get him out, but he couldn't do anything. For some reason, I didn't believe him. I felt that he was lying to me, so I continued to go see George on a regular basis. He was still holding up, and he was still looking good. I didn't think that he would turn into a punk in jail because he was my brother, and he didn't have any sugar in his tank.

The twins were away with Rita at Six Flags, and I wanted to relax, but I had too many things on my mind. I really wanted to go to the shed and find out who or what was hiding in there, but it seemed like, every time I tried to go out that damn back door, someone was always catching me.

Spencer was out on the golf course, practicing his putt. I went into his bathroom and looked through his medicine cabinet. Everything in there appeared to be normal. Then, more shit started rushing through my head. Did his wife really leave him, or did he get rid of her ass? He looked harmless to me, and I wasn't a bit scared of him because I hadn't given him a reason not to trust me. I knew how to play my cards because I had been playing them this long. I went into his closet and sat in the middle of the floor. He had his Steve Harvey suit collection all organized by color. He even had different colored alligator skin briefcases to match each of his suits when he went out of town on business. His Stacy Adams shoe collection was on the other side of the closet, and it was organized by color, as well. I looked at the very top of his closet, and there stood a tall box. When I opened up the box, I found all different kinds of strap-ons in there. He had a lot of different colors and sizes. One was big and brown, and it reminded me of Eric's dick. *What is this?*, I wondered as I held up a butt plug. *He's not plugging that in my ass.* I put it back in the box. *This old man has some serious ass issues if he thinks he's going to fuck me in my ass, too. It's already bad enough that he's fucking me with plastic dicks.*

As I walked deeper into the closet, I saw what appeared to be a small briefcase. I opened it up only to find different kinds of papers. Some were even old newspaper clippings. Others were just insurance policies. One was also his and Jo Ann's marriage certificate. I saw a picture of a woman who I assumed was his wife. If I knew that living the lavish life would be that easy, it didn't matter to me if we got married or not. Everyone seemed to think that he was a killer, but he hadn't done anything to me to make me think that he was crazy. I'd slept with plenty men in the streets. It didn't matter if they were blind or crippled. My pimp made sure I got that money.

"What are you doing in here?" I heard a voice say. I turned around. It was Spencer. I had just put the briefcase back where I found it.

"Hi, sweetheart," I said as my voice screeched. "You startled me. Well, if you must know. I was in here looking at all the different dicks I have to choose from to get fucked with."

"That's the spirit," he said as he picked me up and carried me to the bed.

"Sweetheart, I was thinking we could have sex tonight, not now," I said as I fluffed the pillows under me.

"Whenever is fine with me, baby. I'm just glad you understand me."

I began to get bothered by the newspaper clippings. I wanted to ask him if he did kill his wife, but he had told me not to ask him about his past, and he wouldn't ask me about mine, but his past was a matter of life and death, and mine was just about being a whore.

"Spencer, I have something to ask you, and I want you to answer me truthfully."

"Go right ahead and ask me," he said as he walked and opened the wooden plantation blind.

"Did you kill Jo Ann?"

"No, I didn't. Last year, I was found not guilty. She had moved on. She didn't want me anymore."

"But how could she leave all of this, this big-ass mansion with a maid and a seven-car garage? Not to mention, you are filthy rich. What woman in her right mind would cheat on you?"

Spencer chuckled and said, "You'd be surprised what my handicap would make a woman do. I am so glad that you love and understand me and my plastic dicks."

My mouth is going to get me killed one day, I thought, *because I talk too damn much.* I was the one getting away with murder, but there was something that kept itching at me. I wanted to ask him more questions about Jo Ann.

19
Plastic Dicks Everywhere!

It was nightfall, and I knew that Spencer was looking forward to our night of passionate, plastic fucking. Spencer and I never made love. As far as I was concerned, Eric and I did because we looked into each other's eyes, and we worked up a sweat. When Spencer was on top of me, I could barely look him in his face. It was just something I couldn't do. I really didn't want him to fuck me with those plastic dicks, but what choice did I have? Plus, if I wanted the real dick, all I had to do was go lay up with Eric at my loft. When I got back to Spencer's room, he had already dimmed the lights, and he was playing soft music. I thought, *Dimming the lights is a relief because, last time, the lights were on, and that damn shit bag spoiled everything.* I couldn't stand to look at that space between his legs. He was lying in the bed, smoking a Cuban cigar. *That's ironic. Smoking is probably why he doesn't have a dick now.*

"Come on in here, and join me," he said as he blew a puff of thick, cloudy smoke into the air.

I slipped off my black silk dress and hopped in the bed. I could actually count the number of times we had been intimate. With Eric, I had lost count months ago. I looked at his chest, and the gray and black curly hair that grew there. He wasn't a bad-looking, old man, but he wasn't shit like his nephew in the bed, but I could tell that, back in his younger days, he'd had it going on. I laid on my back, and he rolled over and put the cigar in the glass ashtray.

"This will be a night you'll never forget," he said as he started to lick my nipples.

You got that right, I thought. *How could I forget something as weird as this?* My breasts were my hot spot, and my pussy became moist instantly.

"That's my hot spot," I shyly said as he continued to nibble.

"I told you this would be a night that you would never forget," he said as he slid his big fingers in and out of my slippery pussy.

Then, he focused on my clit and started moving his hand from side to side. My legs were trembling because I was so turned on. Then, I heard a vibrating sound coming from under the thick, fluffy white sheets.

"Are you ready for this?" he whispered as he licked me in my ears.

"Yes," I said as I continued to play with my pussy.

He eased the vibrator in, and it was moving pretty fast. I was surprised at first because I thought that it was going to be cold because it was plastic, and plastic was usually cold, but this felt very lifelike. It was warm, and it was a very nice size. He was on top of me, fucking me fast then slow. I was screaming, and I closed my eyes and visualized that Eric was on top of me. I licked my lips, smiling, thinking about Eric's sexy ass. I didn't know how Spencer got any satisfaction, but he seemed to get aroused by the fact that I was moaning and screaming, "Fuck me, daddy! Fuck me harder, daddy!"

He gave no signs of slowing up or stopping his pace. He could go all night like the Energizer Bunny, so finally, I said, "Yeah. That's it! That's the spot! I'm cummin', daddy, and it feels so good!"

He stopped and rolled over on his back, saying, "I told you I was from the old school. I know how to make you feel good."

He went to clean the vibrator and put it back up. I just laid there thinking, *I can fake orgasms all day and night. He doesn't know if I am faking or not.* When it was all over and done, I needed a damn cigar or a strong puff of some good-ass weed.

"Did you really like my lovemaking?" he asked in his deep voice.

"Of course, I did, baby. I totally understand your situation. You don't have to worry, Spencer. I am a one-man woman," I lied as I held my hand up, showing him the big diamond ring he had bought for me. "I am marrying you for richer or for poorer, for better or for worse."

"That's what I wanted to hear," he said as I laid on his chest. "Speaking of marriage, we're flying to Italy in the morning."

20
Wedding Bells

The next morning, Rita had breakfast ready for us. She threw down, too. She fixed homemade biscuits, scrambled eggs, bacon, Italian sausage, and pancakes.

"This will give you energy," she said to Spencer as she handed him a couple of vitamins.

"See, that's why you've been working for me for over thirty years. You keep me in tip-top shape."

She looked at me and said, "You look like you had a long night, too. Would you care for a vitamin?"

"No," I said as I rolled my eyes and focused my attention on the twins.

They were eating up their food. Even though I was here and there, they still knew who Mommy was. I made sure of that. I made sure to tell them that I loved them every day.

"So, today is the big day," Rita said as she cleared the dishes from the table.

"Yes. It is our special day," Spencer said.

"Too bad I can't fly to Italy with you guys," Rita said, sounding like she was disappointed.

Spencer gave her a suspicious look and said, "What on God's green earth is stopping you?"

"We have a major leak in the back," she said, pointing her head to the back where the shed was.

"I know you can handle that, but I want you at the wedding, so we'll call our friends and get married here at the wedding chapel."

"What!" I snapped. "We can't fly to Italy because of a leak in the back yard!"

"It's really not a big deal. You and I can still fly to Italy for our honeymoon."

"That's more like it," I said as I looked at Rita and rolled my eyes.

Spencer exited the kitchen. He went to call some of his closest friends over. He didn't have any family except for Eric and Evelyn, and I knew that they'd be the first ones to show up.

"Come on, twins. Let's go get cleaned up and dressed for Mommy's big day," Rita sarcastically said as she left the kitchen.

I stood up and walked over to look out the window at the shed. The window on the door was painted black.

"A leak, my ass," I said to myself.

I stared at the shed to see if I could see any movement inside, but there was nothing that my naked eye could see. I wanted to just run back there and open up the door, but that would be a waste of time, considering all the chains and padlocks Rita had strapped on it. *There will be an opportunity*, I thought as I went to get ready for my special day. Spencer was on the phone, telling Walter to make sure he brought Janet along. I wished George could have been there on that day, but that was out of the question, considering his circumstances.

Spencer had planned our wedding in less than two hours. I wasn't surprised because he always got what he wanted. The caterers delivered the most amazing smelling food, and the florist used pretty flowers to decorate the little wedding chapel to the maximum.

I was in my room, putting on the Vera Wang dress that I had picked out months ago for this day. It was a white, knee high gown with a black satin belt that ran diagonally along my waistline.

Rita walked in and said, "You look just like the little angel you are."

I looked at her and thought, *Bitch, I know you don't mean that shit.*

I knew how to put on a front, too. It was not hard to be fake.

"I was there when Jo Ann and Spencer got married almost twenty years ago," Rita said.

I looked at her from under my veil and said, "Is that really necessary? Are you really trying to spoil my wedding day?"

"No, I'm not trying to spoil your day. Besides, you seem to have Spencer wrapped around your pretty, little pinky."

"What is your point?" I said as I clipped on my Bella Crystal drop clip-on earrings with the necklace to match.

"You just remind me of Jo Ann when she first married Spencer. That's all I'm trying to say, but I will change the subject and let you know that the twins are very excited. They're all ready and looking so cute."

She changed the subject just in time because I was about to give her a piece of my mind followed with a fist. Spencer walked in and said, "Sorry to interrupt you, ladies. Are you all having girl talk?"

"Hell, no," I said as I dabbed on a little shimmering pink lip gloss.

"I was just telling her that she and the twins look lovely," Rita quickly said before she walked out of the room.

Spencer looked like a pimp in his Victorian double-breasted tuxedo. It was black and had wide pinstripes with wide legs. I slipped on a pair of Versace heels.

"Isn't it bad luck for you to see me before we get married?"

"No, that's a superstitious tale. Besides, I don't believe in bad luck," he said, looking at me and raising one eyebrow.

"Jasmine hooked your hair up in the nick of time," he said as he touched the ball on the top of my head.

"She sure did," I said as I looked at myself in the mirror. I looked absolutely stunning.

"Come on, sweetheart. We don't want to keep our guests waiting," he said as he grabbed my hand.

We rode the escalator down to the wedding chapel. *There are so many people here,* I thought as I looked around. I saw Eric and Evelyn in the front row. There were very few faces that I recognized as I quickly eyed the crowd. The wedding chapel was huge, and there appeared to be about three hundred people there, including the butlers and maids that Spencer had hired for the day. When Spencer and I stood before the preacher at the altar, I felt Evelyn and Eric's eyes cutting through me. Evelyn always looked at me with her nose turned up, but it was her son that I was fucking, and it was her brother I was marrying. She didn't think I was good enough for Spencer, but that would just have to be a hard pill that her ass had to swallow. I wondered how she'd react if she ever found out about Eric and me. I quickly erased those thoughts out of my head and began to feel knots in my stomach.

I didn't know if I was supposed to shed tears or be just plain happy. The feeling I had was indescribable. Even though I was standing there like I owned the room, the eyes were on me, looking at me in a devious way. I was ready to get it over with. The part where the preacher said, "You may now kiss your beautiful bride," came sooner than I expected because I had drifted off into space thinking about Walter.

I remembered the first time I had gone over to Walter's house. He had a mansion in the same subdivision as Spencer's. Spencer was away on business, and I was thinking about when he said that Spencer had taken Jo Ann away from him when they were in high school. Let's just say I gave him a shot at revenge by sleeping with him.

Spencer raised my veil and kissed me like we'd never kissed before. This kiss was very passionate and real.

"I love you more than you'll ever know," Spencer said as he sealed the last kiss with a smack.

"You guys look great together," Janet said as she and Walter walked over to us. "I can't believe Spencer tied the knot again. I thought he'd be my groom one day," she joked.

I cut my eyes at her because I didn't see how that was relevant at a time like that. It seemed like everyone I came in contact with was very outspoken. Walter grabbed my hand and kissed it and said, "You look like a model. You should be on the cover of a magazine."

He looked me in my eyes like he wanted a round two in the bedroom.

"Let's go have some food and wine," Spencer said as we walked down the foyer to the where the other guests were eating and talking amongst themselves. Eric walked up and said, "Unk, you don't mind if I have this dance with your lovely bride."

"No, of course not, nephew."

As we danced, Eric said, "It's official now. You're married to the mob, and the only way out is death. We could kill Spencer ourselves and get the insurance money."

"Killing Spencer isn't a part of the plan. Why are you being so greedy? I have you put up in my loft. I am giving you money each and every time you have your hand held out. What gives?" I asked as I danced with a huge, fake smile on my face.

I saw Evelyn watching us dance out the corner of my eye. I felt so bad. Spencer really loved me, and I had been nothing but a complete whore. I couldn't believe that he really had feelings for me. No one ever had in the past, not even Bernard. I had to make it right, and I had to get rid of Eric's ass before he killed Spencer.

21
Eric!

It had been a while since I had seen Eric. I was keeping my distance from him. We texted each other on the phone, but I didn't go to my loft anymore. I was trying to be the perfect wife. Right after the wedding, Spencer and I were spending a lot of time together. He had even shown me how to golf.

The twins were well. They were being homeschooled. I liked that better. I didn't see any point in them going to private or public school. We had money, so I hired the best paraprofessionals that Georgia had to offer. I still hadn't had a chance to go into the shed. Rita was like a hawk, watching my every move, especially since I'd been spending more time with Spencer. I missed Eric, but I had to continue to play my cards right until I came up with my own master plan. What I eventually wanted was for George to get out of jail, so he could kill Eric for me. I had never thought about murdering someone before, but it was either him or me.

Spencer was out of town on business, and I was lounging around the room. Rita and the twins were outside in the back yard, running around. I glanced on the dresser and saw a book called *Daddy's Favorite Pop* by Antoinette Smith. I wasn't too fond of reading, but just reading the first page made me want to read the whole book. *I didn't know Spencer read books,* I thought as I flipped through a few pages. I laid down and dozed off before I knew it. I was awakened by my cell phone vibrating on the dresser. It was Eric. I didn't even bother calling back. I just got in my car and headed to my loft.

When I got to my loft, I didn't have to bother letting myself in because the door was wide open, and there was weed smoke everywhere, including in the hallway. The music was loud, and it looked like he was having a party.

"Where is Eric?" I asked Rodney as I unplugged the stereo.

"He's in the back," Rodney said as he plugged the stereo back in the wall.

"Excuse me," I said as I snatched the cord out the wall. "I unplugged it for a reason. This is my damn house, and I want it off right now!"

"Well, excuse me," he said as he flopped down on my very soft, dark chocolate leather sofa.

I looked in the twins' rooms, and, thank God, they were still in one piece. I went to my bedroom. I pulled my fluffy, white comforter back and saw two females in the bed. It was Jade and another girl.

"Where's Eric?" I screamed. "And you, bitches, have five seconds to get the fuck out of my bed."

Eric walked in finally. He said, "Hey, baby. You decided to come and see me. I've been blowing up your cell phone."

The girls grabbed their things and left.

"Eric, what the fuck is going on with you?"

"You know what's going on with me. You got married, and, now, you're trying to cut me out of the equation, but that'll never happen," he said as he held up the disc.

I have got to get my hands on that disc, I thought, *but what if he has made more copies?*

"Eric baby, you have to give me a break. So far, I've been your puppet. What more do you want from me. Killing Spencer is out of the question," I said as I grabbed the sheets off of my bed. "Why did you have them freaks in my bed?"

"You know how Jade rolls. She wanted some pussy, so I let her use the bed."

"Well, you should have let that bitch use the floor."

It didn't matter how pissed off he made me. I would always fall for his trap. I would always give in. Then, we would fuck, and I would forget all about being mad in the first place.

"Look. The plan is going to go like this," he said as he helped me make up my bed with clean sheets. "We can make it look like an accident."

"No!" I screamed. "We are not killing Spencer, and that is final. Boy, this is your uncle we're talking about."

"I know, baby, but think about it. Fifty million dollars would look very nice at the end of the day."

"Can we talk about something else because you are starting to make me feel sick at the stomach?"

Rodney peeped his head in the door and said, "Homey, I'm going to get up with you later. I gotta take these wasted broads home."

"That's where they should have been in the first place," I snapped.

Eric walked back in as I laid on my bed, thinking, *Could we get away with murder? Why should I kill Spencer? He has been nothing but good to me.* I actually visualized myself at Spencer's funeral. I could see myself in a long, black dress with black gloves and black shades on with a black veil. Eric came back in the room, interrupting my vision.

He said, "So, where were we?"

He had a bottle of Hennessey in his hand, and I was surely going to need a stiff drink if he was going to keep on talking about murder.

"Don't be upset," he said as he began to roll a joint. "Baby, you know that I love you, and I don't know what I'd do without you."

He took a drag from the joint.

"Eric, I love you, too, but can we please change the subject for now?"

This boy is crazy, I thought as I poured myself a shot of cognac. Was it possible for me to love two men? Could I love an uncle and a nephew? The more love Spencer showed me, the more I fell for him. What the hell was I doing? Spencer would kill me if he found out I was sleeping with his nephew. I hadn't been a big believer in God, but I needed Him now more than ever, and I needed Him to let Spencer remain in the dark until my plan came into play. I prayed that Spencer never found out about Eric and me.

Eric massaged my neck with his strong hands, and it felt so good, considering all the tension and stress that he had been causing me.

"I really think you should reconsider going to school, Eric. God has given you a talent, and you should use it."

"I told you already. That's out of the question. All the scouts and officials know about me."

"I'm sure, if you were to talk to Spencer, he could get you back in school."

"The main scouts and coaches have already told me that they don't want me because my temper is too bad. Here. Drink some more of this," he said as he passed the bottle of Hennessey to me.

I was starting to feel it. I laid back on the bed.

"Relax," Eric said as he slipped my shoes off.

He began kissing me, and I loved to smell him. He always smelled good. I love a good-smelling man. I started licking in his ear, and he said, "That's why I am so crazy about you. You make me feel like I'm the only man in the world."

I then proceeded to lay him on his back and lick him from his neck down to his dick. His dick stood straight up, and I deep throated it several times before I slid on top. His dick was so hard that I felt the veins in his dick rub the walls of my pussy. Both of our hormones were raging like bulls. It had been a while since we'd fucked, and I had missed him.

"I have a better idea. Let's take a hot bubble bath together," I said as I grabbed for his hand and led him to the bathroom.

He didn't waste any time. He went over to the shower and tested the water, making sure it was hot enough for us both. We both smiled, looking at each other. He was so handsome. I loved his smile and his deep dimples. I especially liked the way he licked his lips like LL Cool J. I looked at his six packs as he ran the water.

"Get over here and finish sucking this dick," he said as the water ran down on it.

I pulled my hair back into a ponytail. I kneeled down and started licking his dick up and down. He couldn't handle it. He was beating on the walls, saying, "Damn, baby! That's why I am in love with you. You can suck the hell out of a dick!"

He made love to my mouth by pushing and pulling the back of my head, hunching me in my mouth.

"Not yet, baby! Please slow the pace down," I said. "I want that hot, healthy sperm in my pussy! Fuck me from the back," I said as I bent all the way over, spreading my pussy wide open.

I thought, *I never want this to end! This is the best sex that I've ever had!*

"Harder!" I yelled as I kneeled down some more, so his dick could go deeper.

He was slapping me on my ass, screaming, "Throw that pussy back!"

He grabbed the back of my neck and fucked me harder until he finally came all in my wet pussy. I was in love with him, and I would have to go to desperate measures to keep it going.

22

Spending Time with My Twins

I was awakened by the doorbell and my cell phone ringing simultaneously. I decided to answer the door and let my cell phone go to the voicemail. I stumbled to the door, holding my head. I didn't remember how I ended up in my bed. All I remembered was Eric and me drinking Hennessey and taking a shower together after having sex. My head was banging. I looked through the peephole and saw that it was Spencer and the twins.

"Hold on a minute, baby," I said as I ran to my bedroom to see where Eric was.

Thankfully, when looked on his side of the bed, there was a note saying that he had left and would be back later. I must say, he had cleaned up the apartment very well. None of his things were in sight. I opened the door, and the twins immediately ran to their rooms to play with their toys.

"Hey, baby," Spencer said as he sat on the sofa.

This was his first time ever coming over to my place. I thought for sure that he was going to check me about something.

"So, what brings you guys by?" I asked as I looked around, noticing that Eric had the place sparkling clean.

"I missed my bride," he said as he tried to kiss me.

I moved away, so he couldn't smell the heavy liquor on my breath.

"Do you want some breakfast?" I asked as I walked to the kitchen.

"No, the twins and I ate breakfast already. You know Rita makes sure we never miss a meal. Besides, she told me that you had left in a hurry yesterday."

"I didn't know she was even aware that I had left. No, I wasn't in a hurry. I just came here to chill out and watch a couple of movies. Baby, let me go freshen up. I'll be back in a flash," I said as I went to my bathroom to take a shower.

I peeped in on the twins before I went to the bathroom. Shelton was playing his video game, and Sherita was on her computer. As I took off my robe, I noticed that I had red marks on my chest. Eric must have been sucking on me, but I did not remember. I grabbed a tube of toothpaste and put some on them, but that didn't help. They only got redder. I had remembered that remedy from back in the day. It didn't work then. I didn't know why in the hell I thought that it would work now. I just stood there for a moment and thought, *When I get out the shower, I'll just cover it up with make-up.* I didn't know what Spencer had in store for me because he was full of surprises. What more could he do for us? We had everything.

I took a quick shower and put on a black silk dress. Spencer loved it when I showed off my voluptuous shape.

Spencer said, "We're going on a road trip."

"A road trip? Where are we going?"

"We're going to the aquarium in Tennessee."

I gathered the twins, and we headed out the door.

"Are we flying?" I asked.

He said, "Road trip. If we were flying, I would have said that we were going to fly."

Although I sensed a bit of an attitude, I didn't say anything. I just cracked a smile and said, "We have an aquarium in downtown Atlanta. Why do we have to go to Tennessee?"

"Because it's good for the soul to get away and relax. Do you know what I mean?"

"I sure do! Well, let's hit the road, jack!" I said as I turned around to tell the twins to strap up in their seatbelts. We rode in Spencer's four-door Cadillac STS.

"Just sit back and enjoy the ride, sweetheart," Spencer said as he put in one of Gladys Knight's CDs.

The song that he played was called "Neither One of Us (Wants to Be the First To Say Goodbye)". I adjusted my seat and sat back and closed my eyes. We arrived in Tennessee in less than four hours. When we walked in the aquarium, the twins were so amazed. I was blown away, too, because I had never seen so many white people before in my life. I felt all eyes on me instead of the damn fish. When some folks looked at me, they directed their attention straight to my ass. I couldn't help that I had a big, pretty, round ass.

"Free Willy!" The twins both screamed as they saw a hump back whale.

"Ooh, Finding Nemo," Sherita said as she glued her face to the glass.

They definitely thought they were watching cartoons. I felt my phone vibrating. Immediately, I told Spencer that I had to go to the ladies' room. When I got to the ladies' room, I opened my phone up to call Eric back. He didn't even say hello. He was mad.

"Why haven't you answered my calls? I've been calling you all day."

"Well, for starters, I'm with Spencer. We're out of town. He came over early this morning, and I haven't had a chance to call you, but I'm returning your call now. What's up, baby?"

"You're what?" he screamed. "When are you coming back?"

"I don't know. Maybe tonight or tomorrow. What's wrong with you? Why are you raising your voice at me?"

"You better not give my pussy to anyone else, and I mean that."

"Calm down. You're the only one I'm sleeping with."

"I know my uncle has tried to fuck you with those plastic dicks."

"No, he hasn't, and how do you know about those, anyway?"

"I know a lot of shit. You just hurry back. I'll be at your pad," he said before hanging up.

I was starting to see a side of Eric that I hadn't seen before. When I caught back up with Spencer and the twins, they were still amazed. We left the aquarium and went to an upscale restaurant. We sat at a private booth.

"My name is Alexis. I will be serving you this evening. What can I start you guys off with to drink?"

"I'll have Hennessey on the rocks."

"Sure. I'll just need to see your identification."

"I left everything at home. I didn't even bring my purse with me."

"I'm sorry. No identification. No booze."

Spencer whispered something in her ear, and her attitude immediately changed.

"Mr. Davis, I didn't recognize you. I'm sorry. Is this your daughter and your grandkids?"

"Hell, no, bitch! Do I look like his daughter?" I said as I held up my ring finger. "Take another wild guess. I'm his wife! Well, since you have my husband's stamp of approval, I'll have the whole bottle of Hennessey," I snapped.

She looked at the twins and said, "What can I get you guys?"

"I'll be ordering for them," I snapped. "They'll have two Sprites."

"Ally, I'll have the usual."

"Sure thing, Mr. Davis," she said as she walked away.

Hmm, he called her by her nickname, I thought, but I was in no position to question anything that he did. I had to figure out a way to fix this mess that I was in with Eric.

"We're ready to order," I said as Alexis came back with our drinks.

Spencer's usual was red wine.

"We'll have three of the nine-ounce filet mignons with loaded mashed potatoes and mixed vegetables."

"That nine ounce is a big steak. Are you sure you don't want to get the seven ounce for your kids?"

"Bitch, did I ask for the seven ounce? If you want a tip, you'll take the rest of our order without any unnecessary suggestions. Now, I suggest you make sure our steaks are well done, or I will clean the floor with your skinny white ass."

She rolled her eyes at me and said, "Will you have the usual, Mr. Davis?"

She seems to know so much about Spencer, I thought as I popped the top on the Hennessey bottle. Spencer had ordered the seafood trio, which included lobster tail crab and shrimp.

"Mommy, we love Mr. Spencer," the twins said at the same time.

"I love him, too," I said as I took a shot of Hennessey.

Alexis came back with our food balanced on plates on each arm. She called out our dishes one by one and placed them in front of us.

"Mr. Davis, I ordered the crab legs just how you like them — cooked in that special sauce you like."

I didn't care if she was one of his old flames that still didn't stop me from going off on her ass.

"Can you send a sister over here to finish waiting on us? Your services are no longer needed."

"There's no need for all of that," Spencer said as he tried to calm the situation.

"There is a need for that. I'm tired of these bitches trying me every time we go out somewhere. Fuck her! And why are you taking up for her anyway? Are you fucking her?" I screamed, but I quickly rephrased that question because he didn't have a dick. "Well, did you used to fuck her when you had a dick?"

"You're acting crazy," he said. "I have friends all over the world, and no one wants to see me get taken advantage of."

"How can I use you?" I asked as I cut the twins' steaks. "How can I take advantage of you when you've given me the world?"

I was pissed off.

"Hello! I'm Tina. I'm your new server. Hello, Spencer, it's been a long time," she said, grinning from ear to ear.

"Hey! I'm his wife, and I'd appreciate it if you toned your friendliness down a bit toward my husband."

"Sure thing," she said, without taking her eyes off of Spencer.

What's with these bitches?, I thought. *I better calm down before I go to jail.*

I excused myself, went to the restroom, and rolled myself a joint. I always kept a twenty with me to calm myself down during situations like that. I was so ready to go. I didn't understand why he took me to places where every bitch in the world knew him. If I didn't have my twins with me, I would have beat both their asses.

"They got me fucked up," I said as I lit my joint.

I was feeling good when I walked back to the table. I imagined watching Spencer fuck both of those waitresses with those plastic dicks. I laughed to myself as I pictured that shit. Tina was sitting at the table engaged in conversation with Spencer. The twins were done, and so was I. We went to sit in the car until Spencer was done. We waited in the car until he finished his nasty-ass seafood delight. I never saw Rita fix that shit at home. I strapped the twins up because we were ready to ride. I rolled up another joint because those bitches in there had really worked my nerves.

Spencer got in the car and said, "You know one drug leads to another."

"Well, if you're insinuating crack, that'll never happen," I said as I blew smoke in his face.

Crack. I will never ever smoke that shit, I thought. I had snorted powder cocaine back when I was working for Money Toney, but I wouldn't let Spencer know that. I didn't like the side effects of it— the running nose, the buck eyes, and, most of all, the paranoia. It had kept me alert when I was tricking. If a trick didn't seem right, I'd move on to the next one.

Spencer fanned the smoke out of his face, and I said, "You need to roll all the windows down because I have about five more joint to go."

23
Back in Atlanta

When we finally arrived back in Atlanta, I was ready to get back to my loft, so Eric could fuck my brains out. I was starting to have mixed feelings about him, but I didn't give a fuck. He made me feel good when I was in his presence, and that was all that mattered.

"I'll take them for you," Rita said as we walked in the door.

She got the twins, looked at Spencer, and said, "Back so soon. I thought you said that you guys were going to be gone for the whole week."

"There was a slight change of plans," Spencer said.

"Yeah, shit didn't go quite like your boss planned," I snapped. "Now, if you'll excuse me, I'm going to change into something more comfortable. I have to go visit my brother in jail tomorrow."

I didn't know what the hell he was thinking, but I wasn't about to be away from Eric for a whole week. I couldn't miss that good lovemaking. I was addicted. My phone was steadily going off, and I knew that it wasn't anyone but Eric.

"Damn it, baby. I'm coming," I said to myself as I slipped out of my skintight dress.

I put on a Bebe shirt and skirt with a pair of Prada six-inch heels. Eric loved to see me in heels. Atlanta's weather was crazy, so it didn't matter what I put on. The night was still young.

"You should at least tell her," I heard Rita tell Spencer as I was heading for the door.

"Tell me what?" I asked as I entered the room.

"It's not a big deal, sweetheart. Please be safe out there and come back to me in one piece."

"I'll tell her," Rita said as she took a shot of vodka and poured Spencer one. "It's your husband's sixty-first birthday, and he wanted to spend it with you and the twins at the cabins in Tennessee."

"Happy Birthday!" I said as I fell into his lap. "Why didn't you tell me?"

I felt kind of bad for showing my ass at the restaurant on his special day.

"Well, sweetheart, I was going to tell you, but you were so caught up in the moment at the restaurant that I just decided not to say anything."

"Rita, can you excuse us for a moment? I would like to have a moment alone with him."

"Whatever," she said as she got up and walked out.

"You better check your damn maid. I am sick of her smart-ass remarks. She always has to have something smart to say. Well, fuck her. I will deal with her another time. Now, back to you and your birthday. Do you want to fuck me with one of those plastic dicks? We can make it quick because I would like to leave from my house, so I can get to the jail on time."

Spencer lived in Alpharetta, and I lived close to the city, which was closer to the jail that George was in.

"You can leave from here. I'll get Q to drive you."

Q, his driver, was an ex-junkie.

"No. That's not a good idea. I want to drive my own car and get some fresh air. You understand, don't you? You bought me a four hundred thousand dollar car, and I want to ride around town in it."

"So, I see you're getting tired of me already."

"No, baby. I'm not, but, if it'll make you feel better, I'll stay the night here with you and leave an hour early tomorrow morning and head to the city."

"That's my girl. That's what I wanted to hear," he said as he turned off the security camera to the back yard.

I knew right then and there that I had made a mistake. Spencer was my husband, but I needed my space at times. He was starting to crowd me, and I was used to going and coming as I pleased. I knew that Eric was at my loft waiting on me. I turned my cell phone off and said, "I'll just have to make it up to him in the morning."

I threw my cell phone on the table.

"So, check this out. Can Q take me to the hood to get some more weed because I am out, and I don't want to drive my car through there. I will need more while you're fucking me with those plastic dicks and that damn shit bag on. Please don't get offended. I'm just saying, when I'm high, it makes the mood right."

"I understand where you're coming from, and I'm sure that won't be a problem. For some reason, it turns me on when you call my vibrators 'plastic dicks'. But it's not a good idea for Q to take you because he's a recovering addict."

He grabbed the keys to his white BMW 745.

"Come on. I'll take you," he said as we headed to the door.

I stood there for a moment, and it was like he almost read my mind.

"What? Did you think I'd be scared to ride through the hood? I know people everywhere. I could go all over this country if I wanted to."

"You proved that to me today," I said sarcastically.

Well, he didn't know about my brother George because he would have been robbed by him.

"If it'll make you feel better, I'll bring this with me," he said as he walked to the closet and grabbed a .45 caliber.

"It looks like a John Wayne gun," I said.

"I feel like John Wayne," he said as he put it in a holster.

"Spencer, please be careful," Rita said as we walked out.

"We're good. You just make sure my twins are good, nosy-ass bitch."

She nodded her head as she closed the door.

"Spencer, what's with everyone? Why is everyone so overprotective of you? I'm sure you will leave her well-compensated when you die as well since she takes such good care of you, huh?"

"With Rita, it's not about the money. She's very loyal, and she's been with me through some very rough times in my life."

"Well, did you fuck her when you had a dick?"

"No, but she was there when my wife walked out and left me for a younger man. She was there when I had my surgery. She cleaned the catheter bag every night in the beginning."

"You mean that shit bag."

"Yes, that shit bag," he said, getting irritated. "That shit bag has a name."

"I don't care what its name is. It looks disgusting, and you better not leak any of it on me."

"I have everything under control. Has any ever gotten on you in the past?"

"Hell, no, and thank God because, the day that it does, you'll be fucking a blow-up doll! Good. Now that we got that out of the way, I really need a joint and some crack," I joked.

"I understand your reaction. My wife was the same way, and she left me. End of story."

"With all that money you have, why can't you go and buy another dick?"

"Because it's not that simple," he said as he hit the steering wheel. "Now, will you just drop the subject please?"

He was getting pissed off, and all I could do was think about him saying, "Whatever you do, just don't make me mad."

Well, she was stupid. There is no way in hell I'm leaving his rich ass, I thought.

"Take a left right here on Bankhead. I would go to the Bluff, but their bags are too skimpy."

"Do you need to take this in there with you?" he asked as he raised the chrome pistol in the night light.

"No, definitely not. I know just about all these bastards around here, but, if I'm not out in five minutes, you can come in blowing motherfuckers' heads off," I said jokingly.

"What's the password?" a junkie asked as he opened the main door, leaving the burglar door locked.

"Crack! Now, open up the damn door, you crack head motherfucker!"

"Wrong. Guess again?"

"If you don't open this door, I will kick you in the nuts with these heels when I get in there," I said as I wiggled the door knob.

"Give me your money, and I'll go get what you want."

"You must be a damn fool if you think I'm going to give my money to a crack head."

By that time, G-Man came to the door and opened it up. G-Man was my old pimp's right hand man and cousin.

"You know your pimp is down the road, and he's never getting out."

"Good," I said. Then, I asked for a pound of weed.

"Come walk with me this way," he instructed.

As I walked through, I realized that this was a real crack house. Junkies were shooting up dope with needles, and some were smoking crack pipes.

"Who is that pretty, little thang you got with you?" one of his homeboys asked G-Man. "Oh, shit! Is that George's little sister?"

G-Man turned to me and said, "Word around town is you caught that rich, old, crazy cat who cut up his wife and made her ass disappear. I saw him a few times, and I wanted to put the steel to him, but he always has a million bodyguards with him and shit. I'm not going to try and trick you because I know you know your drugs. Plus, you was my cousin's bottom bitch."

"You damn right," I said as I snatched the weed and smelled it. "How much do I owe you?"

I sniffed it like it was some Downy fabric softener.

"That one is on me if you turn around and let me see that fat ass. You still fine as fuck," he said as he grabbed his dick. "My office hours are from nine to five when you get tired of that old dick. When you want to get that pussy beat down by a beast, you know where to find me."

"Nigga, please. I am a married bitch, and I don't fuck with dope boys. I fuck with six digit figure niggas, niggas whose cars ride without keys. I fuck with niggas who have mansions."

"Well, I hope you got some insurance on that old bag because he don't have much time."

As I walked out, I could have sworn I saw Keisha's face, and, if that was her, that explained why he gave me the weed. That was my brother's dope.

24
Riding in the A-town

When I got back in Spencer's car, he was listening to Marvin Gaye's "Let's Get it On". Just the thought of getting it on with him made my stomach turn. He was handsome and all, but the thought of those plastic dicks and the shit bag was just too damn much for me, but this was my life, and I had to put up with him until he croaked. I hoped it would be very soon.

"Did you get straight, baby?" he asked as he bobbed his head to the song.

"Yes, indeed. I got some California weed. See how green it is and how loud it is when you smell it. This is the good shit. Niggas die over this shit every day."

He turned the music up, and it sounded so crisp and clear. It sounded like Marvin Gaye was singing in the back seat. Why did Marvin Gaye's daddy have to kill him? I guess some parents really believe the saying, *"I brought your ass in this world, and I will take your ass out."*

"This is my jam," he said as he continued to nod his head to the beat.

I would have rather listened to Rick Ross, Jay-Z, or Lil Wayne. Hell, I would have rather listened to Gucci Mane, and I hardly ever understood anything he rapped about, but he had a lot of hits, and I loved the beats to his songs. Plus, he was from the hood. *Anything but that slow-ass music right now,* I thought as I rolled myself a fat-ass joint. I let the seat back and started humming along with the song.

"If you'd like, sweetheart, we can just ride around and listen to this good music."

"That's fine with me. Do you have any plastic dicks in here because I don't want to be fucking all outside and shit. I don't get down like that."

I was lying through my teeth. When I was working those streets, I would fuck them tricks just about anywhere. We'd fuck anywhere from McDonald's bathrooms to the filthy AAMCO bathrooms. It didn't matter. If they were paying, then I was laying.

"You know I got more respect for you than that," he said as he held up my ring finger. "We can ride around and look at the stars."

He pulled into a neighborhood park.

"Don't they look so peaceful," he said as we both glanced at the sky. "When the good Lord takes me, I know that he has a place for me in the sky. I'm going to be a shiny star."

"I used to wish that same shit when I was younger. As I got older, I wanted to die and come back as a bad piece of crack. I wanted my mother to smoke it, so I could bust her heart wide open."

I started to tear up because she wasn't a bad mother. She was just never there.

"Don't be so hard on yourself. I'm sure your mother has her reasons," he said as he rubbed my thighs.

"Had her reasons, as in past tense, because she's dead, and the funny thing is that her body was never found. It's fucked up how she died and left me to defend for myself in these rough-ass streets. It's a jungle out here," I said as I knocked the ashes off the end of the joint and into the ashtray.

Spencer looked like he wished that there was something that he could do, but all of his money and all of Oprah's money couldn't heal my heart.

"There were some things that I really needed to learn from her, like when I first started my period. I didn't know what to do, and George told me to put on a washcloth. My brother has always been there for me. That's why it's so important for me to visit him and try to get him out of that place. Since you know everybody, how come you can't pull strings and get him out?"

"Like I told you, he is a three-time convicted felon, and it's up to his parole officer."

"Well, can't you pay her off or snap your fingers?"

"Not with her, she's the type that makes examples out of our young black men. It's good to cry. That's a self-healing process," he said as he kissed my hand.

I thumped the end of the joint out and looked up at the stars through the sunroof.

"I'll do everything that I can for your brother. Just try not to dwell so much on your past. It will kill you. Trust me. I know," he said as he looked up at the sky.

He acted like he felt guilty about something. I didn't know exactly what it was, but I knew that something was bothering him. I didn't know what he meant, and I didn't want to know because I already had enough shit to deal with.

"I think we should just go back home. I will run you a hot bubble bath. I want you to just relax. No plastic dicks," he smiled as he cranked up the car.

"That sounds like a good idea if your ass isn't joining me," I mumbled under my breath.

"That sounds just dandy," I said as I cracked a fake smile, "because talking about my family has gotten me down and salty."

"No problem. I am going to pamper you and watch you sleep all night."

"That sounds like a plan to me," I said as I strapped on my seatbelt.

That strong-ass weed knocked me out before I knew it. I was awakened by Spencer carrying me into the house. While he was carrying me in the house, I saw Rita coming in from the back door. I was going to make my way out there that night. He laid me on the bed. Then, he went to run the water and light candles all over the room and bathroom. I looked down the hall to make sure that the coast was clear. I tiptoed to the kitchen, and I looked out the window first. Then, I reached for the back door. Just as I was about to open the door, I felt a hand grab my shoulder. Then, I heard Spencer say, "There you are. You must be sleepwalking. Your water is ready, sleepy head."

He picked me up and carried me upstairs. *There will be another time,* I thought as I stepped into the steamy tub. I knew that he and Rita were hiding something back there. I sat in the tub, thinking, *What in the world am I going to tell Eric since I'm not making it home tonight?*

25
Eric's Crazy Ass

When I woke up the next morning, I heard the twins ripping and running as they played in the hallway. Spencer was in the bathroom, shaving. I was still in the bed because my head was spinning. The aroma of the breakfast that Rita had cooked was good, but I couldn't stomach it. I didn't have an appetite. I had a hangover. I needed some tomato juice or something that would coat the acid in my stomach.

"Good morning, sleeping beauty. You were resting so peacefully. I watched you all night."

"Do you happen to have an Alka Seltzer around here?"

I was holding my stomach. Spencer turned and walked to his bathroom.

"And while you're at it, please give me two headache powders as well," I called as he walked away. Then, I said, "Oh, shit! What time is it?"

I thought I was late for George's visit. I was relieved when I reached over and looked at the time on my cell phone.

"I got everything you need," Spencer said, returning to the room.

I looked over at the fifth of Hennessey bottle, and my head began to hurt even more. That bottle hadn't shown me any love.

"I feel like shit," I said as I went to brush my teeth.

I smelled like a walking alcoholic. My head was spinning, and it didn't help when I brushed my teeth. I gagged and threw up everything. It was nasty, but I felt better.

"I was trying to tell you to slow down," Spencer said as he handed me a cold washcloth.

"I bet you and your plastic dicks had fun with me last night."

"In all honesty, you were so upset. The more you talked about George and your mother, the more you drank, so I didn't bother you. I thought I made that clear last night."

I knew Eric was somewhere going crazy. He got cranky when he didn't hear from me. After getting dressed, I kissed the twins and told Spencer that I would get up with him later.

"Sure you will," Rita said as she held the twins' hands and had them say, "Bye, bye, Mommy."

There that bitch goes again with those smart-ass remarks, I thought. I saw straight through her fake ass, and, if she wasn't fucking Spencer, she sure did act like it at times. When I was heading to my car, I saw Q outside, washing Spencer's stretch Cadillac limousine.

"How do you do, ma'am?"

"I am not an old-ass lady, so you don't have to use that form of expression with me."

"It's only a form of respect, ma'am."

"Well, use something else," I said as I popped the lock on my Maybach. "You can call me Queen."

I put on my black Versace shades. Then, I turned to him and said, "And don't you forget it."

He turned his head with an attitude and continued washing the limo.

"Queen, I have orders to drive you to the city," he said as he turned to me.

I felt eyes watching me, and I was right. Rita was looking at us through the window.

"Fine," I said as I stormed into the limo and slammed the door shut.

"Here. Pop this CD in. I'm tired of listening to that old shit. And that's an order."

I handed him a mix CD with different rappers on it. Listening to that music made me want to ride through the hood and find Keisha and beat the hell out of her. There was a song on there called "Knuck if You're Buck," and I was definitely buck.

"You might want to roll that window up. I'm 'bout to burn it down back here," I said as I showed him a Ziploc bag of weed.

I was in a zone. I was feeling the music, and I was feeling a good high. Suddenly, I felt the car stop. We were at a Seven Eleven gas station.

"What the fuck?" I asked as I looked out the window and over my shades.

He rolled down the window and said, "Queen, I have to take a leak."

"Hurry the fuck up! I told you that I have places to be! First, we have to stop by my loft. Then, it's off to see my brother."

He pounded his fist on the door and said, "Look! I have been nothing but nice and respectful to you. Now, you either show me some respect, or this limo is not moving, and you will miss your 'places to be'."

He turned and walked off.

"Who the hell do you think you're talking to? I will have your job terminated in the blink of an eye," I yelled at his back.

When he returned, he got into the car confidently. Then, he turned in his seat and asked, "Have you adjusted your attitude?"

"Yes, sir," I said as I blew thick weed smoke into his face, "because I realized that I can have you fired. You'll be unemployed by tomorrow."

Then, I rolled the window up.

"I'll always have a job," he said once he had rolled the window back down. "You have no idea who I am, do you?"

"No, and I don't care. Spencer told me that you're an ex-junkie."

"Well, that's true, but did he, also, tell you that I am Jo Ann's son?"

I started shaking and felt like I was about to piss on myself.

"So, tell me. What's stopping an ex-junkie and a three-time convicted felon from choking the breath out of you right now?"

I swallowed and said, "Whoa! I am not the enemy here. Spencer is."

"He is the enemy, but he, also, loves you very much. He loves you just like I loved my mother. She was harmless, and she didn't know anything but love. She sure as hell didn't deserve to die."

"How do you know that she's dead? He could have her hidden somewhere."

"Hidden for ten years!" he screamed.

"It's possible," I said. "I see stuff like that on the news all the time."

"I am just waiting on the right time to make my move," he said as he grinned while he was getting back in the limo. "So where to, Queen?"

"To my loft downtown," I said as I regained my composure.

As soon as we approached my building, I saw Eric running towards the limo. I knew, just by looking at the expression on his face, that it couldn't be good. The car hadn't even come to a complete stop when he opened the door and snatched me by my hair, saying, "Why haven't you answered your cell phone?"

"You know that I love you, Eric, but I am married to your fucking uncle, so what do you expect?" I said as I kicked him in his nuts.

"Oh! You done fucked up now," he said as he fell down to the ground.

I looked at Q. He just sat in the car. He didn't even stop Eric from slapping me in my face or pulling my hair. I didn't care if he was Jo Ann's son or not, he'd have hell to pay for letting Eric put his hands on me.

"You wait until I catch my breath, bitch. I am going to kill you," Eric said.

I ran into my house and retrieved my baby Desert Eagle. I waited for him to come into the house. I had fought too much in the ghetto, and I wasn't about to get my ass kicked by a young-ass nigga.

"Where you at bitch?" he said as he threw the door back so hard that he put a hole in the wall as the doorknob slammed through it.

"I'm right here," I said as I put the gold-plated gun in his face. "Now, I suggest you calm the fuck down."

I cocked the pistol back.

"What has gotten into you, Eric?"

"You is what has gotten into me. Oh, you're going to shoot me because I'm in love with you, bitch!"

"No, I'll shoot you if you ever put your fucking hands on me again. Besides, if this is your love, I don't want it."

I had never shot my gun before, but Spencer had always said, "Before you shoot, make sure the safety is off. Then, you just point and shoot."

"Okay, baby. We're both pissed off, so let's just calm down. Please let me get some ice for my nuts," Eric said.

"Eric, I wasn't pissed off at first, but I am now. Look at my face. I can't go visit my brother like this. You punched me in my lip, and it's swollen."

"I'm so sorry, baby. I don't know what came over me. I've been in this house for two days. I wanted to hear your voice."

He walked over to me and grabbed the gun out of my hand. He put the gun on the countertop and said, "Can you please get me some ice for my fucking nuts?"

I said, "Can you please get some ice for my fucking lip?"

We smiled at each other and headed to the kitchen.

"Go sit on the sofa. I will get the ice," I said as I opened the freezer. "Lay back. I'll do it for you."

I pulled his jeans off.

"What were you going to do with that gun? Were you really going to shoot me?"

"If you ever put your hands on me again, you'll find out, and we'll just leave it like that," I said as I eased the ice on his nuts.

"If I had acted like I was scared or backed down, I'd probably be a bloody pulp right now."

Fighting Eric was like getting into a fight with someone in the hood. They never really knew your fighting skills, but they could sense fear based off of your actions. I didn't win every battle that I fought, but I did win most of them.

As Eric laid back on the couch, he looked like he was in a lot of pain.

I put some ice on my lip, too. I knew I wouldn't be going to see George because, if he'd seen my lip, he would have probably broken out of jail to kick Eric's ass. I knew that I couldn't go see him like that. I went outside and signaled for Q to leave.

"I'm sorry, baby, and I will apologize to your brother, but I thought that you had gone on with your life without me."

"There's no need to apologize to my brother because he's never going to find out."

"Well, for what it's worth, I'm still sorry, and I mean that from the bottom of my heart."

For some reason, I believed him.

"Eric, it's only been two days since I've last talked to you. How could you think such a thing?"

"I know, baby, and I'm going to make it up to you."

"Eric, the only way you can make it up to me is by getting rid of our sex tape."

About ten minutes went by, then there was a knock at the door. I looked out the peephole, and it was Q.

"I told you to leave," I said as I opened the door.

"Come on in, homie," Eric said as he straightened up on the sofa.

"So, what's the plan?" Q said to Eric.

"The plan is going into play real soon."

"Wait a minute! You two know each other?" I said, closing the door.

I was very confused.

"Yes, we know each other. He is Jo Ann's son."

"And this is Eric, the adopted child," Q said as he laughed like it was so funny.

"Adopted?" I said as I sat on the sofa next to him. "You mean to tell me that Spencer isn't your real uncle?"

"Hell, no, and that damn lady Evelyn isn't my real mother, either," he said as he gave Q a high five.

"So, when were you adopted? You really had me fooled."

"Let's just say that I was at the right place at the right time. I was playing basketball one day, and Spencer saw potential in me. I never dreamed of that basketball shit. I've always wanted to be a boss."

Now, I knew why he wanted to kill Spencer so fast. He wasn't his blood uncle.

26
Laying Up in the Rain

I knew I needed to make a move, and I knew I needed to make it quick. I needed to get George out of jail, so he could help me get rid of Q and Eric's asses. I could go to the hood and pay some junkies to off them, but they'd only get high and start running their mouths, so they couldn't be trusted. I could only trust my brother. I hoped that he was doing okay in jail because, from what I had seen on TV, the bigger guys always ruled over the smaller guys. George was small, but he had heart. He was a gangster, and I knew that he could take care of himself in there. I just hoped he didn't get in more trouble in there and get life before Spencer could make a move and get him out.

It had started to rain, and I mean hard. Q had left, and Eric was still laid across my lap, holding the icepack on his nuts.

"Baby, I want to fix us something good to eat," he said as he removed the icepack from my lip. "The swelling is going down. I am really sorry for punching you. Do you forgive me?" he said as he stood up to stretch.

He looked like he was still in pain.

"Yeah, I forgive you. Have your nuts stopped hurting yet?"

"No. If you had a pair, you would know how it felt. They're still a little sensitive, so I need you to lick them for causing them to go into distress."

I looked at him with one eyebrow raised and said, "Boy, you crazy. I'm not licking your balls with my busted lip."

"I was only joking," he said as he walked into the kitchen.

"Where's your Corvette?" I asked.

Eric had bought himself several cars with the healthy allowance I was getting him out of Spencer's safe. One in particular was a gray Corvette with red stripes going down the middle.

"The engine blew," he said as he took out some rib eye steaks.

For some reason, I felt like he was lying to me. That was a brand new car, but it was so damn hard for me to be mad at him. He was so good-looking; he looked as if he could be on the cover of GQ magazine.

"What do you know about cooking?" I said as I flipped through channels on the TV.

"I know as much about cooking as you know about guns," he joked.

"I'll eat whatever you cook as long as it's done."

When it was all over and said and done, he had fixed steaks smothered with onions and mushrooms with loaded mashed potatoes and broccoli. It was good. The steaks were seasoned just right, to perfection. The broccoli wasn't too hard or too soft. It was just right, and the hot, buttered mashed potatoes were creamy and well-beaten with no lumps.

"I'm impressed," I said as I took a sip of white wine.

"I am a jack of all trades," he said as he rubbed his chin. "I'm a lover, fighter, gangster, and one great cook."

"Speaking of that gangster shit, can you please call off whatever it is that you're planning against Spencer? He has cancer for crying out loud."

"He doesn't have cancer. Is that the lie he's been telling you? He's never had cancer. Jo Ann cut his dick off. She cut everything off, including his balls. The lacerations were too deep, so they couldn't sew his dick back on, and there was no saving it. I would have killed that bitch, too, if she had cut my dick off," he said as he drifted off into space.

That explained the weird look that Spencer had down there. I felt bad for him.

"Why did she cut if off?"

"She cut it off because he beat her ass and she was tired of his shit. She would catch him cheating, and he would get mad at her and beat her ass for confronting him."

He's not going to beat my ass, I thought as we chilled and watched *Weeds. Weeds* was a TV show about a suburban white lady who was a drug dealer. It was one of my favorite shows. That white lady really got off on those drugs. I hated that my boy U-Turn was cancelled off the show because he added humor to it, but I guess that was Hollywood. Once you get used to seeing certain familiar faces, they just go away without any warning.

Eric started caressing my neck and asked me if I could rent a Lincoln Navigator for him. My first thought was no because I only had credit cards, and they belonged to Spencer. So far, I had covered my tracks pretty good.

"I don't see why that should be a problem," he said as he rubbed my back.

I felt his dick poking my back. I don't know how we ended up on the floor, but, before I knew it, his dick was in my mouth.

"Yeah, deep throat your dick, baby," he said as his toes curled. "This dick belongs to you and only you."

I was slurping and burping at the same time. I was so horny and turned on. I was licking the tip of his dick in a circular motion. He was fucking me so hard in my mouth that it felt like he was touching my esophagus. I didn't gag, though. I handled that dick like a professional whore. I was moaning his name and juggling his balls in the palm of my hand. I enjoyed watching him feel good. I loved pleasuring him. His dick got really hard, and I knew that he was about to explode, so I stopped and turned over for him to fuck me from the back.

"I want it hard. I want you to slap my ass and pull my hair."

I loved having rough sex with Eric. I was dripping like a running faucet. I felt like I had already caught an orgasm while I was sucking his dick. I loved sucking his dick, and the more I sucked it, the hornier I got. He shoved his hard, throbbing dick in my pussy and grabbed my neck and said, "Who's pussy is this?"

"It's yours, baby, all yours. Baby, I love you so much."

"I love you, too, baby," he said as he slapped my ass hard.

He was my young, crazy nigga that had stamina, and I was his older chick who fell for his charm and loved it. I had never been in love before. I never loved Bernard's sorry ass. I wasn't in love with Spencer, and there were even moments when I didn't love myself, so how in the hell could I be in love with Eric? I came to the conclusion that we were crazy in love, and the definition of it was whatever we wanted it to be.

27
Doing Time Alone

I rented the Lincoln Navigator over the phone for Eric. I had Q to pick me up and take me to Spencer's to get my Maybach. Neither one of us spoke about what had happened the other day, but I had made up in my mind that I would definitely respect him, considering the fact that Spencer had something to do with his mother's disappearance. I didn't even go in. I just got in my car and headed to go see George. I made a quick stop at the car wash, and I saw some familiar faces, looking at me as I got out of my Maybach. As I got closer and saw the onlookers, I spotted Keisha. When she saw me looking at her, she immediately took off running.

"You can run, but you can't hide, bitch!" I screamed. "I will catch you and beat your ass!"

I gave the detailer my keys. It was funny how the baddest bitch in the projects was running from me.

As I left, I let the sunroof back and popped in BIGG DOGG FEE's CD called *Cut The Check*. He was a rapper from Savannah, Georgia. To me, he sounded like a rapper from New Orleans but better. I loved to listen to his slang. I thought, *He is going to blow up one day.* His music made a lot of sense to me. It was basically what every other rapper was rapping about, and that was trying to make it out of the hood. I could have listened to his CD all day. He had a song on his CD called "Shooter." His image fit his voice because he was a tall, slim, dark-skinned, and handsome rapper. He reminded me of Eric, at times. I bet he had a big dick, too. I promised myself that, when he came to Atlanta, I was going to show him some love and check out his performance. I loved listening to all these different rappers tell their struggles, which was the same, but it was in their own words. I loved that shit. FEE was definitely a talented rapper.

While I was riding, I realized that I needed a serious vacation away from everyone. I was just worn out. Between Eric, Spencer, and the twins, I felt drained. When I'd have sex with Eric, sometimes, it was like fucking sixty niggas. He'd fuck me dry sometimes, but he made sure that I caught multiple orgasms. Sometimes, when I'd cum, he'd lick it and share it with me by putting his slippery fingers in my mouth and playing with my slimy juices. We were both freaks. We'd have sex whenever we felt like it. We had sex in the parking lot of McDonald's one day. We didn't care. There were people walking by, watching the car move, but we kept on fucking like dogs. I was his poodle, and he was my pit bull, fucking me doggy style.

When I got to the jail, all eyes were on me once again, and I must say that I loved the attention. There were several officers trying to open my door at once.

"Thanks you, guys," I said as I ran my fingers through my wrapped hair.

I was looking good. I had on a Michael Kors v-neck sweater dress that stopped right above my knees with a pair of Michael Kors heels to show off my thick calf muscles. The lady officer enjoyed frisking me. She rubbed her metal scanner against my breasts slowly. Then, she ran it up and down my legs slowly, doing it one leg at a time. It was clear that I didn't have anything, considering what I had on. *The pistol is in the car,* I thought. The only metal that buzzed her metal detector were my diamond earrings and necklace.

"Right this way," she said as she opened the door that led to my brother.

I ran to him and hugged him. He was shackled from head to toe.

"Can you please take these off?" I asked as I held up a crisp one hundred dollar bill. "So, how have you been?"

I continued to hug him.

"I'm good, lil sis. You know I'm gonna be alright. I see you're still lookin' fly as usual," he said as he stepped back, looking at me from head to toe. "You look like money."

He grabbed my arm and looked at my platinum Rolex.

"Yes, George, I must admit that life is great."

"You still got that old cat by the nuts?"

Yep, I thought, *and Eric has me by my clit.*

"Let's just say I am playing this deck of cards until you raise up out of here. How are they treating you in here? Are they trying to rape you and shit?"

"Hell, no," he quickly said, "and if any fucking goes on in here, I will be the one fucking, not the one getting fucked. These guards and niggas in here know my history. They know not to try me. I'll kill one of these marks in here."

He mean-mugged a guard.

"Well, I am working to get you a good criminal lawyer on the outside, but it's hard because your parole officer is a bitch."

"She's a racist bitch," he added. "I appreciate the money that you keep stacked on my book."

"You practically raised me, so that's the least I could do. Today, I was getting my Maybach detailed, and I saw that bitch Keisha, and she took off running."

"Wait a minute! You have a Maybach?"

"Hell, yeah, and I have a white two-door Bentley coupe. Anyway, I have a feeling that Keisha has given your drugs to G-Man because I went to go buy a pound of weed, and he didn't even charge me."

"Sis, you got to get me out of here," he said with rage in his voice and eyes.

"I am doing everything I can to get you out because I am in a bind, and I need you to eliminate two niggas for me. Well, really just one, and his name is Eric. I think that I am in love with him, or it could be lust. I don't know how to distinguish the two."

"Well, baby girl, you can't be in love with him if you want me to kill the nigga."

"Well, maybe you're right. I have to figure this thing out. I messed up by sleeping with Spencer's nephew. Now, he's blackmailing me. He recorded us having sex and is threatening to show it to Spencer if I don't do what he asks of me, but he says he loves me, and we have this crazy love/hate sex relationship going on."

"Sis, you have a lot on your plate, and I hate that I am not out there to help you out. You better find that bitch Keisha before I do because, when I raise up out of here and find her, I'm going to kill that bitch. Now, back to this nigga Eric. What in the world possessed you to sleep with him in the first place?"

"I don't know. I was caught up in the moment. I enjoyed it, and we kept doing it."

"I'm not the smartest man in the world, but, if you're taking care of him and he's still blackmailing you, then he needs to be dealt with. It doesn't take a rocket scientist to figure that one out."

"You're probably right, but I got myself into this mess, and I will get myself out."

I didn't want to tell him too much of my crazy life because he might have started a riot in there.

"All I can do is take it one day at a time in here. I live by the word every day. Although, I am a gangster, I really believe that God has a place for niggas like me in heaven. I really believe that God has a special place in heaven for us killers and drug dealers and adulterers," he emphasized.

He started talking some deep shit. He scared me because he sounded like he saw death around the corner.

"I read my Bible faithfully. All I have is time on my hands, and all I can do is read. Oh, speaking of reading, I heard that there is a hot, new author on the streets, and her name is Antoinette Smith. She has a book out called *Daddy's Favorite Pop*, and, from what I heard, it is a must read."

"What a coincidence!" I said. "Spencer has that same book on his dresser at home. I don't have time to read it, but I will make sure I bring it to you on our next visit."

"Please don't forget. I also heard that she has a new book called *Married: Sneaky Black Woman*."

"Really that sounds like me," I said as I looked at my watch.

"Time sure has passed."

We had been talking for almost two hours. This was the part of the visitation I hated — watching the guards shackle my brother up like he was an animal.

"I love you so much," I said as I stood up and hugged him with all of my might.

"I love you, too, sis, and keep doing what you're doing to get by until I get out. And tell the twins that their uncle loves them, and I'll be out soon."

"I will give them your love. I will continue to stay on Spencer because he knows so many people, and I'm sure there are some strings he can pull."

I began to tear up because he was getting ready to go back in there and be housed with all types of criminals. I didn't care if he did belong there. He was my only brother, and I wanted him to be in the free world with me.

28
Spencer's Connects

When I left, I immediately called Eric and told him that I was going by to talk to Spencer and that I would be home later. These two relationships were getting the best of me, but I juggled them like two oranges. When I pulled up at Spencer's, he wasn't in the house. I thought, *This is the perfect time to go sneak in the backyard and look in the shed.* I didn't see any sign of the twins or Rita. I opened the back door, and there they were, playing on the playground in the backyard.

"Spencer's on the golf course," Rita screamed.

Just when I thought I was going to finally find out what was in the shed, there she was right in front of it. I walked out there and kissed the twins. Then, they ran and started swinging on the swings.

I drove my car to the golf course.

"Hey, baby," I said as I got out and straightened my dress out.

He was on the golf course with a few of his friends and all of them looked like money.

"Hey, gal! I've been missing you," he said as he picked me up and spun me around.

I felt them looking at me with blank stares. Then, they started whispering to one another. I got a pretty good look at each and every one of them just in case I saw them on the street somewhere. I never really had the opportunity to meet his friends because, during our wedding a few months back, the only face I remembered was Eric's, and that was because we had fucked on the terrace. Spencer was dressed in his Polo golf attire, and he looked nice. He looked like he could have been my granddaddy, but I didn't care. I loved it when we were out together in five star restaurants, and I ran shit. I loved to see the older chicks' faces crack when they found out that I was his wife and not his daughter. I wasn't a celebrity, but I felt like one. I could go anywhere and buy anything I wanted. It was just that simple.

"So, sweetheart, have you found my brother a good lawyer?"

"As a matter of fact, I did. That is him standing over there with the burgundy shirt on. Go on over there and say hi. He's already been filled in," he said as he hit the golf ball.

As I walked over to talk to him, my breasts shook with each step I took. I felt them looking at me like hungry werewolves.

"Hello. I'm Sherman Goldstein," he said as he extended his arm to shake my hand. "I have your brother's file right here. George Michael Smith, and he has several different aliases. He's also known as King George."

"King George?" I asked as I looked at the papers in the manila folder.

"It seems that your brother is a wanted man in New York and California."

"That's impossible because my brother has never left the state of Georgia."

"Are you sure about that?"

He showed me mug shots of George in New York and California in his teenage days.

"But he was only a kid. How could they get him for that?"

"That doesn't dispute the fact that he was a runner for a kingpin named Ice. Ice is from Columbia. He has distributed cocaine all across the map. No matter what, your brother always done what he told him to do. Ice told him to follow out a hit on a rival drug dealer, and he's been under his wing ever since. King George was his right hand man, but he's wanted for several other felony charges including rape and kidnapping. The best I can do is talk the judge into giving him seven years fed time."

"Seven years!"

"Yes, seven years. He's looking at life according to his rap sheet. When you go see him on his next visit, tell him to accept the seven years. Tell him not to crank up the jury because, if he does, he'll get up to sixty years."

My eyes grew bigger, and I said, "No one can do sixty years!"

"There are prisons full of men who are doing hard time, and some of those men have died in there. So, if you don't want to see your brother die in there, tell him not to crank up the jury. Since you're Spencer's beautiful, young, sexy wife, I will do this free of charge."

I didn't know if that was a good thing or a bad thing. He, then, gave me a firm handshake, but I wasn't finished talking. I was still stuck on the fact that he told me that George was wanted for rape.

"Who did my brother rape?"

"I don't know who he raped, but it looks like he hasn't been convicted of it just yet. When we're young, we tend to get ourselves in things that we will later regret in life. They will come back to haunt us."

Don't remind me, I thought as my past reflected in my head along with Eric's face. When I was in the streets, it was pure hell, and I thank God that I am disease free because I had fucked and sucked plenty dicks. I walked away feeling sad because George had to do seven years in prison. There were so many crazy people in prison, especially the ones that were serving life sentences. They didn't care about killing another inmate in there. I was having all types of mixed emotions. I left Spencer and his buddies on the golf course. I went to look for my twins. When I walked in, there was no sign of them. I went into the kitchen and looked out the window at the shed. Spencer was only a few feet away on the golf course. I decided to be nosy another time. I went back to the golf course. As I looked on, Spencer and his buddies were wrapping things up. He kissed me and said, "You want to fool around a little bit. You know you're always so busy, and, now, it seems that I hardly see you."

I thought, *I haven't drunk enough Hennessey yet, and I have to be dead-ass drunk to fuck you.*

"You look so sexy," he said as he kissed my neck.

On the way to his room, I grabbed a bottle of Hennessey from the bar. I hated to get fucked by those plastic dicks, but a girl's got to do what a girl's got to do. It didn't take much to please him. All he wanted was a little quality time. I had my own place, money, and cars. The least I could do was lay up with him when he wanted me to. It couldn't get any better than that. He seemed to understand that I was younger than him and that I wanted to do things like club and hang in the streets. To me, he was just a humble, old man.

When we got to his room, he went to his closet and said that he had a surprise for me. I thought, *What? Do you have a bigger vibrator?* He handed me a key pad that didn't have keys on it. It only had the letter "B" on it. He told me to turn around, and he covered my eyes with a scarf and led me to the garage. When we got to the garage, he took the scarf off and, to my surprise, I was standing in front of a black, two-door Bentley coupe. On the front, it read "Spencer's Girl".

"Thank you so much, baby," I said as I hugged him. "What more could a girl ask for?"

"I'd give you my heart if you needed it," he said with a serious look on his face.

We were interrupted by the doorbell. It was Eric. And from the look on his face, he wasn't happy. I looked out the door, and the truck that I had rented for him was wrecked. *What the fuck*, I thought.

"What's up, Unk?" he said as he looked at me.

"You're what's up," Spencer said. "Where have you been? Your mother has been worried sick about you."

"You know how it is, Unk. You were young once. I've been seeing a woman, and I am in love with her."

"Is that right?" he asked as he lit his Cuban cigar. "I would love to meet her someday. Well, it's no secret that you're not going to the NBA. Did you think I wouldn't find out?"

"I was going to tell you, but I knew my mother would tell you first. I'm having fun and enjoying my life. I don't have to go to the NBA. I have a wonderful woman who is taking good care of me."

"You were well on your way to being the next LeBron James."

"I know, Unk, and you don't have to remind me of that every time you see me. I am in love, and it feels good."

"Well, I hope she's worth your future and your career."

"As a matter of fact, she is," Eric said, looking at me.

I felt very awkward. I excused myself and walked outside to get some fresh air. I wondered, *What the fuck is he trying to pull?* I was so nervous. I could only hope Eric didn't spill the beans. I just prayed that he loved me like he said, so he would keep his mouth closed about us.

29
Come on, Unk

When I walked back in, neither Spencer nor Eric was in sight. His mansion was so huge that you could really get lost in there. I figured that Spencer was probably in the shower. He had worked up a sweat on the golf course. I went back to the garage to look at my Bentley. When I got out there, Eric was in the car. When I walked up to him, he said, "I am going to look real good driving this."

"What the fuck happened to the Lincoln?"

"Oh, it was nothing but a minor fender bender."

"Do you know that Spencer will find out about us if the insurance company calls him?"

"Well, it looks like you better get down there and pay for the damages before he finds out."

"What happened? Were you in a hit and run accident? If so, where's the police report?"

"There is no police report. I was drunk, and I hit the median leaving Magic City."

I knew right then and there that Eric didn't care about our relationship, but I did, and I cared about us. I was just as crazy as he was for putting up with all of the nonsense that he was taking me through.

"Oh, yeah, and another thing. Since my uncle is going to start popping up at your loft, I need you to get me my own spot. I need you to get me a condo."

"Get you a what?" I said as I fell to my knees. "Go home and live rent free with your mother."

"Baby, you said you loved me, but, if you want me to be at your loft when Unk shows up, then so be it."

"What are you kids out here talking about?" Spencer said as he walked up, drying his head with a towel.

"We're out here talking about this Bentley you bought for your lovely, faithful wife," Eric said.

"Baby, why are you on your knees?" Spencer asked. "Are you okay?"

"Yes, I am okay, baby. I am so overjoyed about my new ride."

I wondered if Spencer had heard any of our conversation.

"You see, Eric. If you had stayed in school and focused on your goals, you could do the same for your girlfriend."

"Unk, to tell you the truth, I plan on doing just that. I need you to give me that twenty grand because I am going to invest in a business proposition."

"This is ten," he said as he threw Eric a gold envelope from out of his robe.

"You won't be sorry, Unk," he said as he left.

"You gave him ten grand just like that?"

"It's not a problem. He's going to invest in a restaurant. I talked to Evelyn, and she thinks it's a good idea."

"I have to run an errand," I said as I just remembered to get the wrecked car to a place to pay for the damages. "I love you, and I'll be back shortly."

"I love you, too," he said as he watched me ride away in my new Bentley.

I immediately got on my cell phone, called Eric, and told him to meet me at my place in twenty minutes.

"I'm already here," he said before hanging up. I stopped at the rental car place and paid nine hundred dollars in damages. I told them that I would return with the Navigator shortly.

When I got to my place, Eric was laying on the sofa, counting the money that Spencer had just given him.

"What are you up to? What are you going to do with that money? You're not going to invest in any restaurant."

"You're right. I'm not. I'm going to buy me a kilo of cocaine."

"Eric, we have to stop seeing each other for a little while. This is beginning to get too risky."

"This isn't over until I say it's over," he said as he grabbed my keys to my new Bentley. "I have to go and take care of some business. You can take that truck back. I don't need it anymore. Oh, yeah, and don't forget to pay for the damages."

He laughed and kissed the keys as he walked out the door. I sat back on the sofa in tears because Eric was showing his true colors. He really didn't give a fuck about anything, not even himself! I grabbed the keys to the truck and headed to the rental car place.

"Back so soon?" the lady said as I walked in.

"I won't be needing this anymore."

"Do you need a ride because we can assist you with that?"

"Damn," I said as I slapped myself upside the head. "Can you please call me a taxi?"

When the cab driver pulled up at Spencer's mansion, he was shocked. He asked me if I was someone famous. I thought, *I will be famous if Spencer finds out about Eric and me.*

30
Lying Only Leads to More Lies

When I walked in, Spencer was gone. *Perfect,* I thought, *I can just jump in my Maybach and leave.*

"Did you just get out that cab?" Rita asked.

"Damn. You scared me," I said as I turned around.

"What happened to the Bentley Spencer bought for you."

"You knew about that?"

"Yes, I'm the one who picked it out."

"Umm, it's at my place in the garage."

"You can fool Spencer, but you can't fool me," she said as she gave me an evil look.

"I don't know what you're talking about, and, if you want to keep your job, you will stay the fuck out of my business."

"Sweetie, Spencer will never get rid of me. I was working for him long before you were ever thought about. I've seen your kind, and your kind doesn't last long. Oh, and, by the way, I've been teaching the twins their ABC's, and the only word they seem to know is Eric," she said as she walked out.

The nerve of that bitch. Does she know about us? I felt weak at the knees again. I had so much shit going through my head. I wished I could do away with my problems like they did on TV. *Just kill them all,* I thought. I felt in my heart that Rita was hiding something, but, if she did know about us, she would have let it be known, or would she? She hadn't bit her tongue thus far. She probably didn't know, and she was probably trying to pull my card and make me tell on myself, but that would never happen. I vowed that I would go to my grave without anyone knowing about the shit I had done.

I hopped in my Maybach and headed to the weed spot. I wanted to see if I could catch Keisha there. When I pulled up, something was different about the house. They had a drive thru window, so you could drive up, order your drugs, and keep it moving.

That's cool, I thought. *I don't even have to get out of my car.*

But I was on a mission, and it was to find Keisha. She might have thought that she'd gotten away with stealing George's drugs, but I was determined to find her when she least expected it.

"What do you want?" a dope boy asked as I drove up.

"I want to see G-Man," I snapped back.

"Hold on. I'll go get him for you. Wait a minute. You're that girl that is married to that old, crazy-ass man."

Everybody seemed to know that Spencer was crazy but me. He was cool, and I didn't see any signs of craziness. To me, he was a free-hearted, old man.

"What's up, baby?" G-Man said. "Are you ready to give me some of that pussy?"

"Hell, no! I am looking for Keisha. Have you seen her?"

"Don't try to act all sophisticated now. You're the same bitch that used to walk up and down this street and sell ass for a living."

"I did that because I was young and dumb and I needed a place to stay."

"Well, Keisha don't be over here all the time. She stops by, and she keeps moving. She brought me a clean lick, so I have to protect her."

"Is that right?" I said as I sucked my teeth.

That let me know for sure that she had taken my brother's drugs.

"She caught a nigga slipping and brought me his work."

G-Man never did know when to stop talking. I would just have to stake out this place in an unmarked car because they had security cameras everywhere. *Either way it goes, his ass is going down,* I thought as I sped off.

When I got back to my place, Eric was not there. All I could do was hope he didn't come back with the Bentley wrecked. *At least, I can sit back and get high in peace,* I thought, *but where could he be since he claims that I am the love of his life?*

I turned on my favorite television show *Weeds* and started thinking about how everything had just turned upside down for me. *I can't erase my problems, but I can smoke them away for now,* I thought as I lit a joint. I laid back, enjoying my high feeling. I felt like I could touch the moon. I felt like I didn't have a care in the world, but I knew that I was up a creek without a paddle.

31
Thinking Back

When I woke up the next morning, I was thinking that I should have never slept with Eric, but I felt that I was in too deep. Spencer was a great guy who didn't deserve my evilness and selfishness, but he couldn't fuck me like I wanted to be fucked and Eric could. I needed a vacation. The twins and I could fly anywhere I wanted us to go, but I had too much on my plate right then.

After I got up and fixed me something to drink, Eric came stumbling in the door. My first instinct was to look out the window at my car. I saw a girl sitting on the passenger side.

"Who the fuck is that?" I asked as I threw a pancake box at him.

"She's nobody, just someone I have working for me. Come here, baby. I missed you," he said as he hugged me.

For some reason, I felt in my heart that he was lying about that girl. *Everyone had to be the fool sometimes*, I thought. *Look at Spencer. I'm playing him for a fool, and he doesn't even know it.*

"Where are you coming from?"

"We just left an afterhours spot on the West Side."

It was nine o'clock in the morning, and he expected me to believe that lie. He looked like he was high off of something other than weed. When he was high off of weed, his eyes were usually slanted and red, but, this time, they were wide open. He looked like he'd been using some of that kilo he had been talking about buying. A person who did drugs or used to do drugs could always peep another person who was on drugs.

"So, when are you going to get me a condo? The sooner, the better," he said as he grabbed a brown paper bag from under my kitchen sink.

The doorbell rang. Then, the girl who was in my car just walked on in.

"Can I use your bathroom? And where is Eric? He don't need to be leaving me in no damn car! I have to pee," she said as she wiggled her legs together.

My first thought was to slap her ass and watch her piss on herself for walking into my house. She was loud, and she was drunk, too. She had on a pink halter top with a pair of cut off shorts and a pair of pink pumps. *Worker, my ass,* I thought as I shut the door. *I know he's fucking her.* The same way Spencer let me be free and do things was the same way I was with Eric.

"I thought I told your stupid ass to stay in the car?"

"First of all, if this is your sister, how come I have to sit in the damn car?" she hissed back.

"What kind of games are you playing?" I asked as I watched her find her way to the bathroom.

"Look, baby. When you left me those few days, she filled in for you. She reminds me of you."

I didn't see how she reminded him of me. She was flat-chested, and she didn't have a big ass like me.

"What the fuck did you say? Can you run that by me again? You got that bitch in my car, and now she's pissing in my house!"

"Just hear me out, baby. She works for me, too. She holds the drugs for me, and she sells them for me, too. I love you and only you. She don't mean shit to me."

I knew he was playing me, but what could I do? I was in love with his young ass, and I didn't know how to fall out of love.

"You have a nice-ass place here," she said as she flopped down on my brown suede sofa. "So, you're going to be my sister-in-law."

She looked around the living room. Then, she said, "We're getting married, and I can't wait."

"Bitch, you talk too much. Go wait in the car, and I will be out there in a few."

"No, don't be in such a hurry. How long have you guys been together?"

"We've been together since middle school. Then, I moved with my aunt and lost contact with him. I was so glad that we linked back up. I was going crazy without that dick," she answered.

The more she talked, the more my blood boiled.

"I don't know if I should tell you this, but your brother has the prettiest dick I've ever seen. I just love it when he talks dirty to me while I'm riding him."

I was so mad. I wanted to shoot both of them.

"Samira, you're drunk, and you need to shut the fuck up before I put my foot in your ass," Eric angrily said.

I was so mad, and I couldn't do anything but listen to her brag about how good his sex was. He grabbed her by her neck and pushed her out the door.

"Go! Wait in the fucking car!"

I didn't know what I was going to do, but I had to stop this fucked up relationship that Eric and I had going on.

"Baby, I love you, and she's just a fling. Don't be mad at me," he said as he kissed me on my neck.

He had a way of saying things that made me forgive him instantly. I knew that she was probably his girlfriend on the side, but I was, too, and I was in love with him.

"Eric, I understand you're young, and you have raging hormones, but, if I ever see that bitch in my car again, I won't be so nice the next time."

"You'll never see her again," he said as he walked out the door.

32
Sugar Mama

I got Eric a condo just south of Atlanta. It had been a while since I had seen him. I was staying at my home, and I knew that he was with that bitch in the condo that I got him. Eric was still doing the same old shit. He was selling drugs and having different bitches in my cars, but all we'd do was fuck, and I'd forget about it. I knew Spencer was lonely. It had been months since I'd seen him, but, as long as he had Rita there, I knew that he was good. The twins knew more about Eric than Spencer. When Eric and I used to have sex, they would hear me scream his name loudly.

I decided to pay Eric a little visit. I felt like a sugar mama. Not only did I furnish his condo from top to bottom, I also paid the rent up for a year. I even had a fish tank installed in the wall with all sorts of fish in it. When I got there, I laid in his bed and called him to come there and chill with me. He walked through the door, saying, "I don't have time to lay up."

"Why not?" I said as I opened up the window and saw that bitch in my car.

"I have to take care of some business. Next time you want to come over, call me first."

"I have to call you, and I am the one who got this place for you."

"Can you just respect my mind?" he said as he added baking soda to a Ziploc bag of cocaine.

"So, you're going to have that bitch over here?" I said as I put on my clothes.

"There you go worrying about the next bitch."

"As long as I take care of you, then you have nothing to worry about. Look around," I said. "I am the one taking care of your ass. All you can do is make me cum, and I can find another nigga to do that for me."

"You're not crazy enough to fuck around on me."

I went as far as opening up a bank account and keeping plenty of money in it. He must have thought I was a damn fool.

"I will come over here when I feel like it."

I have my own set of keys, so how can he stop me? I thought. We both walked outside, and I popped the lock on my Maybach.

"Hey, sis," the bitch said. She had her feet propped up on the dashboard in my car. I ignored her and sped off, leaving tire marks in the street.

While I was listening to the radio, I heard that there was this place where you could go read poetry. It was called Open Mic Night. I needed to get away and relieve some stress. I went to my condo, took a shower, and put on a long, sleek black gown with a pair of gold stilettos. I was dressed like a queen. I pulled my hair up in a ponytail, letting my bone structure light up in my face.

When I arrived at the café, I used valet parking and walked in. I felt like I was making a grand entrance at the Oscars or something. I definitely felt overdressed as I saw everyone else in casual gear. I wasn't shy, and, as I looked around, I saw all types of people.

"Welcome to Open Mic Night."

I heard the familiar voice say. She looked very familiar to me, but I could not remember where I knew her face from.

"I'm your host Bianca, and this is the place where we never judge you. We embrace and love you. Whatever talent you have, come on up and show it off. If you sing, dance, or rap, come on up and bless the mic."

When I went up there to sign my name on the list, I remembered where I knew her from. She was the sales person at Phipps Plaza.

"Hi," she said as I walked up to sign in. "You're Tameka, right?"

She handed me an ink pen.

"Yes, and I remember you, too," I said as I signed my name.

"I could never forget you," she said, looking at me from head to toe. "You're wearing the dress."

She had her eyes glued to my perky breasts.

"Thank you," I said, realizing that she was coming on to me.

She was gay, and I had known it when I first saw her at Phipps Plaza.

"Whatever you want will be on me," she said.

"No, thank you. I am good. I have my own money."

"Don't be so defensive. Let me take care of you tonight."

"If you insist, then I guess so."

"That's more like it," she said while twisting her dreads. "So, what are you going to be doing tonight? I know you're not going to dance in those high heels."

"I am going to do a few poems."

"I wish you were going to dance. I'd love to see that," she said as she licked her lips.

"We'll see," I said as I winked my eye at her.

She walked me to a table and ordered me a bottle of Hennessey. She walked back to the mic and said, "We have a full house tonight, and it doesn't matter if you're straight, gay, or bi- sexual. We're all going to have a good time tonight."

Bianca had on a Polo outfit with the boots to match. She was a very attractive stud.

"You know how we do this each and every week. I will go first and warm things up. For those of you who know me, you know that anything will roll off of my tongue. And for those who don't know me, you will love me," she said as she looked at me. "This is a poem called 'It's Okay to be Gay'."

It's Okay to be Gay

I'm gay, and it's okay
Hell! You might be bi, so why lie?
Who's to judge you and say that you'll go to HEAVEN or HELL?
Listen to me. Live your life, and live it well.
People will say this, and people will say that.
They're the ones who don't know where their hearts are at?
You know what you want, and you've made up your mind,
So forget all of the stares. You'll be just fine.
Who's to say that you will be judged by that on Judgment Day?
God loves us all in His own special way,
And that's my perspective on being gay.
Ladies tried dick, and men tried clit,
Neither one was a match. It just didn't fit.
So, as long as you're happy, and you can see
That you made your choice abundantly.

She got a standing ovation. I stood up and clapped for her, too, because I thought that she had done a great job. That was a really nice poem, and she wasn't afraid of her lifestyle, and I didn't knock her. She came over to my table and sat down.

"That was nice," I said as I sipped on my drink.

"Thanks, but that was just a warm up. There's plenty more where that came from. I always speak about my lifestyle because I am gay and proud of it. I love being gay," she said as she poured herself a drink. "Remember this," she said as she handed me a picture of us. She still had the picture that we had taken when she helped me try on my gowns. When I looked at the picture, I looked so happy. Now, when I looked in the mirror, I saw bags under my eyes. Eric was stressing me out.

"So, how have you been? I've been thinking about you ever since we met."

"I've been good," I said as I watched the next poet go to the stage.

"I'll be right back," she said as she went to go introduce the next person.

"Everyone give it up for Tee. How are you guys doing out there tonight?"

Bianca's eyes sparkled from the stage. Then, she handed the mic to Tee.

Tee said, "I will be saying a poem called 'I'm Bi. Why Lie?' "

I'm Bi. Why Lie?

I'm bi. Why lie?
Ladies, don't knock it until you give it a try.
Maybe, I'll only be like this for one night,
Or maybe for the rest of my life.
You guys look at me like I'm crazy in the club
When I kiss her on the mouth and give him a hug.
Well, I'm not crazy, and I know what I want.
I want a guy and a girl. I can't front.
Two women, to me, is hot and sexy,
Just having fun and being so messy.
She's creaming over here, and I'm creaming over there.
She likes the excitement of me pulling her hair.
When I'm with him, I want both of them.
I did just that and went out on a limb,
So I finally got all three of us together.
We made a tornado, making our own stormy weather.

There was sweet sweat, & I'll never forget.
The three of us together, I'll never regret.
I was licking her clit as he was hitting my pussy from the back.
She said, "Yeah, keep licking it fast just like that."
He busted in my ass, and she busted in my face.
We fell asleep and woke up and did an instant replay.
I love her legs, and I love his eyes.
Hell, I'm crazy in love with both of you guys.

She dropped the mic and walked off of the stage like she owned it. I had to close my mouth. I was overwhelmed by how descriptive she was. My pussy had gotten wet while she was talking about the creaming part. She didn't look bisexual, but how does a bisexual person look? She was sexy. She was a tall glass of milk with cream added. She was light brown, and her hair was long and black. It hung down her back. I stood up and clapped for her. That was absolutely amazing.

"Give it up for Tee, everybody," Bianca said.

The next person to go up was a short, light-skinned girl, and she looked very young.

"Hello, everybody, you all know how emotional I am, so please bare with me. For those of you who don't know me. My name is Kym."

She cleared her throat and opened up her paper and said, "This is a little something that I put together. Everyone who knows me knows that I've been to hell and back. I love to speak poetry. It helps me forget about all the bullshit. It also helps me to get some of this pain out. So, here we go. This is a poem called 'You Can't Relate'."

You Can't Relate

You can't relate to the shit I'm about to say,

Unless you've walked in my shoes for damn near a day.
When I was growing up, I never had a mom,
And, by age 13, I was good at making different men cum.
I had my first child when I was 14 years old,
And her daddy was never around. His heart was so cold.
A year later, I gave birth to my second daughter.
Her dad and I would never make it to the altar
His mother – God rest her soul – taught me interesting things, like how
to cook.
A year later, I had a son by a known crook.
The thirty dollars that he gave me for child support
Was a waste of my time, showing up in court.
My son could never buy anything exquisite.
All he really wanted was a father/son visit.
By the time I was twenty, I'd given birth to another son,
But fighting with his daddy was a fight that I never won.
He used to beat me, turning me black and blue,
But getting my ass beat
When I caught him cheating was something that I couldn't get used to.
Again, a year later, I gave birth to my last child,
But his daddy was so verbally abusive that I rarely had a chance to smile.
He was a trick in the beginning, and he still is to other girls today.
When I met him on Simpson Road, I wished I would have looked the
other way.
When I found out that my mom had me by her step-daddy, it really had
me shook,
But, despite that fact, she was brave because my life she could have took.
She said that my grandma wanted to raise me for herself.
She wanted to raise me as my mama's sister, or my mama had to face
death.
When I finally found my daddy in California to hear the truth,
He admitted to what he did, and that was my proof.
He was 28, and my mama, his step-daughter, was only 14,

But the truth, that he was wrong, I guess he'd never seen.
I can't be mad at him. Otherwise, I wouldn't be here,
And, besides, I have 5 precious kids that God gave me that are so dear.

She was in tears when she was done, and I was, too. I felt her pain. I started thinking about my childhood. I felt like I knew her. I could relate to her because I had never had a mother, either. I had to get myself together. I went from feeling horny to crying. I mean I was sobbing, and I was the only one crying. Everyone else must have been used to her style, but I wasn't, and she touched close to home with me.

"Hold your head up," Bianca said to Kym. 'You know we love you, and we got your back. Everybody, give it up for the next poet. Everybody has to give her a warm welcome. This is her first time here. Give it up for Tameka!"

That's me, I thought as I stood up, feeling the cognac. I walked up there, and I was drunk. I was past tipsy. I looked at the bottle. There was only a corner left. I walked up there thinking that I was going to be nervous. After listening to everybody else's poems, I thought, *I can do this.*

"Hello, everyone! My name is Tameka, and I won't be long. I have just a little something I want to get off of my chest."

I eyed the crowd as the lights shone in my face. All sorts of things were going through my head. I wanted to say something about Eric and Spencer, so I decided to freestyle and say whatever came to mind.

"Here goes," I said as I took a deep breath and began to let my soul speak freely.

I don't know why I continue to sleep with him.
He's not good for me, but I love him.
His sex is so damn good,
And his uncle got me out the hood.

Sleeping with my husband is a total waste,
But, sleeping with his nephew, I have to keep up the pace.
I knew that it was wrong from the start,
But I wanted him to be a part of my heart.
No one knows our secret, and it is so fun.
I love it when he makes me cum.
Now, he's brought another bitch into the equation,
And he's keeping her. There's no persuading.
There is no one but myself to blame,
And I hate myself that I am in love with a lame.....

33
Flipping the Script

When it was all over and done, I felt like I was with family in there. They liked my poem, and I think I gave everyone in there my phone number. As we mingled and continued to have a good time, Bianca never left my side. She insisted that we hang out some more. It was still early, so I didn't see why not. I knew Eric was somewhere with his bitch.

"You did a good job up there," a drag queen said to me. "You did very well for that having been your first time."

He turned and proceeded to twist his way out the door.

"Let me wrap things up," Bianca said as she pushed the chairs up to the tables.

While she was cleaning up, Kym came over and struck up a conversation.

"You're messing with a no good man, huh?" she said as she sat down.

"As a matter of fact, I am, and I want to get out of it at times. Then, there are times that I want it to last forever."

"That's why I love this place. You can say whatever you want, and no one will judge you," she said. "I have a lot of pain inside, and there's so much more."

"I feel you," I said as we high-fived each other.

"Well, I have your number, and I will keep in touch with you. Are you coming back out next week?"

"Are you kidding? This is now my second home," I said as I got up.

"Are you ready?" Bianca asked.

"Yes. I am. I was talking to Kym. We seem to have a lot in common."

"I've been telling her to leave those no good-ass men alone and switch to the other side," Bianca said to me, while looking at Kym.

"The other side isn't any better," Kym said. "Being in a relationship with a woman is no better than being in a relationship with a man. I've seen that with you and the crazy women you deal with. What am I supposed to do? Take a woman home and tell my five kids, 'Listen up! This is your step-mama.' Hell, no. I don't roll like that. That gay shit isn't for me, but I still love you," she said as she left.

I checked my cell phone. I had no missed calls, not even from Spencer. I couldn't believe that Eric hadn't called.

"Are we taking your car or mine?" Bianca asked.

"You can ride with me. Is that cool?"

"So, how are you and Mr. Davis doing?"

"We're doing good."

"You're doing damn good," she said as she walked to my Maybach.

I put on some soft music as we headed to the South Side. I pulled up at Big Daddy's Catering in Riverdale.

"Oh, my God! This place has the best soul food in the world," Bianca said.

"I know, right? The food here is to die for, especially the slow cooked oxtails over rice, macaroni and cheese, and collard greens," I said as I parked.

"Girl, I love this food, too," she said. "I always get the tender turkey wings with rice and dressing and cabbage."

We walked in, and we both spoke to Big Daddy and his son Marcus. The waitress, Peaches, sat us down and brought our food to us.

"So, I see that life is treating you good."

For some reason, I knew that she was going to start talking about my life.

"I see that you look so good on the outside, but how are you feeling on the inside?" she asked as she poured hot sauce on her turkey wings. "While I was listening to your poem, I heard you say that you were sleeping with Mr. Davis's nephew."

"Yes and no," I said as I sipped on my iced tea.

"What do you mean 'yes and no'?"

"I mean I need to cut it off, but it's too late. I don't want to talk about him right now."

"Well, let's talk about me," she said. "I had a girlfriend, but she was stripper, and you know how that goes. I was in love with her, but she wasn't in love with me, so now all I do is spend time hosting Open Mic Night."

"You're not working at Phipps anymore?" I asked.

"No, I'm not. I didn't get a chance to thank you for that generous commission you left me. I want to thank you now."

"You're welcome. Well, to me, it looks like you found your passion."

"I want to be the first gay girl rapper to represent for the lesbos. I have a lot of gay shit I want to drop."

"I feel you," I said as I pushed away from the table. I was stuffed with oxtails.

"I want you to hang with me and see how we get down on the other side. Have you ever been to a gay club?"

"No," I quickly responded.

"Well, you don't have to look like that. We're harmless. It's no different from a straight club. A lot of women want to try this shit, but it's not for everyone. I am a fool with this tongue. I have had married women to leave their husbands over this tongue."

"I'm scared of you," I said as I backed up.

After we left Big Daddy's, I dropped her off at her car. We were going to meet up later. As I drove away, I couldn't help thinking, *Can I fit a woman into my equation?*

34
What the Fuck?

I stopped by my house to change clothes. I decided to wear Polo. I didn't want to stand out like a sore thumb. I was a bit overdressed in the long dress and heels I had on. I put on a white polo t-shirt with a pair of navy blue polo shorts and a pair of plaid polo skippers. I wasn't jazzy, but I was comfortable. Besides, I could get jazzy whenever I felt like it. I stopped by Spencer's to check on him and the twins.

"Mommy! Mommy!" my twins said as I opened up the door.

My twins were getting so big. Shelton was starting to look more and more like Bernard's sorry ass. I hugged them both and kissed them.

"Where's Spencer?" I asked Rita as she walked in. "He's out of town on business."

I didn't care. I was glad he wasn't there.

"I sure do miss him," I said loud enough for her to hear.

"I bet you do," she said as she walked off.

I knew that she would have something smart to say, but I didn't let her smart remarks bother me anymore. I had gotten used to them. She was a good sitter, and she was taking care of my husband and my twins. She hadn't hurt them, and, as far as I was concerned, she was no threat, just a lonely, old maid. She was just miserable and got her rocks off by getting smart with me. I played with my twins for a while before I headed to Bianca's.

I stopped by my house again because I needed to grab some more money. It wasn't like I needed any, considering that Bianca was treating, but I stopped by anyway. *You could never have too much cash,* I thought.

When I opened the door, I could tell that Eric had been here. It smelled like weed and three-day-old fish. I immediately opened windows and lit candles and sprayed air freshener. I opened up my bedroom door and saw people having sex in my bed. I thought, *I know Eric is not that damn crazy to have that bitch in my bed.* I turned on the lights and pulled the covers back, and, to my relief, it wasn't Eric. It was a girl and a boy that I had never seen before.

"Who the fuck are you, and why the fuck are you in my bed? Get the fuck up and get out before I shoot both of y'all!"

The girl jumped up and so did her perfect breasts.

"Shawty, calm down! Eric said that it was okay for me and my girl to chill here!"

That was it. Eric had pulled the last and final straw.

"This isn't Eric's place, so get the fuck out! It is not cool for you and your girl to chill here, so grab your things and get the fuck out!"

I was pissed off and the girl seemed to be disoriented or something. She got up and walked to the bathroom naked. She looked Brazilian. *She is fine as hell,* I thought. She mumbled something as she walked away.

"Are you his friend from school?"

"Yes, I am his friend Cameron, and we both got caught up and our NBA contracts got cancelled."

"Your girlfriend is too pretty to be smelling like that," I said as I held my nose.

"That's not her pussy smelling like that. She tried to cook some fish, and she burned it."

"What?" I said as I ran to the kitchen.

I was relieved to know that it wasn't her pussy that was smelling like that.

"Look! We can just settle this by calling Eric," the Brazilian girl said.

"Bitch, are you deaf? We don't need to call Eric. This is my place, not Eric's! Now what you need to do is get dressed and get the fuck out," I said as I stared at her neatly shaved pussy.

She had a bad-ass shape, and I was getting turned on by her curves. I didn't know whether to be mad or enjoy the peep show.

"You don't understand. We don't have a ride."

"Get Eric on the phone," I said as I lit a cigarette.

I didn't smoke cigarettes, but I grabbed one of his and fired away. I was so pissed off. They didn't even respect my bedroom. They had ashes and beer bottles everywhere.

"He didn't answer from my phone. Maybe, he will answer for you," Cameron said.

"So, are you really a sugar mama?" the girl asked as she lit a cigarette.

"A what?" I said.

I almost choked on the thick smoke.

"Eric has been telling everyone that you're his sugar mama. He also said that he had some dirt on you, and you're going to take care of him for the rest of his life."

While she was talking, Cameron walked over and slapped her in her mouth and said, "Bitch, if he wanted the bitch to know all of that he would have told her himself."

"Look, whatever the hell your name is! Y'all have five minutes to get out of my shit!"

"I don't appreciate you calling me a bitch," the girl said.

"Look, shawty! That's how I talk. I call my mama a bitch at times," Cameron said.

"Shawty, get the fuck out," I said as I mocked his slang.

"We're gone, and Eric said that he'll deal with your ass later," he said as they walked out and slammed the door.

I couldn't believe this shit. My loft was fucked up! They had shit everywhere! I got on the phone and called a cleaning service. While I was waiting, I took the sheets off of my bed. Under one of the pillows was a Ziploc bag full of ecstasy pills. I called Eric. He answered and said that he would be at my place shortly. He sounded like he was pissed off, but he couldn't be more pissed off than I was. I didn't know what I was going to do once I saw him. I was so mad at me. How the hell could he let his bum-ass friends fuck up my place? Why did he tell them I was his sugar mama and that he has dirt on me? I needed a drink. I went in the kitchen to get a beer and found that those fools had drunk them all up. I sat down and rolled myself a joint. I needed some relief because I felt like my head was going to explode. I flipped on the TV and turned to *Weeds*.

I had been watching TV for a while when Eric finally walked through the door.

"What's up, baby?" he said as he walked over and tried to kiss me.

"Don't fucking touch me," I said as I got up and looked outside to see if he had that bitch in my car. If she would have been in there, I was going to catch a murder charge because I felt like killing somebody.

"Why in the hell did you let people come to my place? Look at my place! It's all fucked up!"

"Please don't be mad at me. I thought that you went out of town with my uncle."

"Well, didn't you call me to see if I was or not? No," I screamed before he could answer the question. "And why are you telling people that I am your sugar mama? And why are you telling people that you have dirt on me?"

"Hold up! Give me a chance to answer you. Now, first of all, I thought that you were out of town. Secondly, I told that dumb-ass nigga to clean up behind himself."

"Well, why didn't you let them to go to your place?"

"Because I don't want everybody to know where I live."

"But you want them to know where I stay? Is that it, Eric?"

He came closer and reached for the joint and took a puff.

"Calm down, baby. You're just paranoid. I love being with you. I wasn't thinking clearly when I let that clown-ass nigga and that slut come over here. I'll make it up to you. Do you forgive me?" he asked as he blew smoke up my ass.

That was a bunch of bullshit, and I had to get that disc and get rid of it. There were times when I knew that he was lying to me, and this was one of those times. I would just watch his eyes lie. I was in love with his great sex. I was in love with his big dick. I was in love with him pulling my hair and slapping me on my ass. I was in love with my man's nephew. We did the usual— smoke weed, fuck, and make up. I'd forgotten about everything, even that bitch. To me, out of sight was out of mind. I knew I wasn't the only one he was fucking, but he made me feel good when he made love to me. I loved the way he licked in my ear and moaned my name. I loved the way he sucked my pussy. His lovemaking made my legs shiver, and his dick left me speechless at times. I believed everything that he told me. I didn't know why, but I did.

"I need some money," he said as he wiped some sweat from his forehead.

"How much do you need?" I asked, hugging him and not wanting to let him go.

"A couple of hundred," he said.

I went to the closet to get it for him. He kissed me on the cheek and told me that he loved me. It sounded right at the time, and I believed him. He left, and I saw him get on the passenger side of my Bentley. There was a bitch driving my car, and I thought, *Spencer is my fool, and I am Eric's fool.*

35
The "Other Side"

My loft was back to looking brand new thanks to the cleaning service. I was ready to go with Bianca to the gay club, and I was down for whatever. I took the pills and put them in my pocket. I got in my car and headed to Bianca's house.

When I pulled up, she shouted out the window and told me to park and come inside. She lived on the East Side in Decatur. When I walked in, a man was on the sofa, and he said, "Are you a femme or one of those boy bitches?"

"I'm neither," I said with an attitude.

"Come on back here. That is my Uncle Pete. He asks everyone that same question, but he is my uncle, and he took me in when my parents put me out. When I told them that I was gay in the seventh grade, they kicked me out. I never liked boys," she said as she sprayed on some Fahrenheit cologne. "We're going to have fun tonight," she said as she lifted up a Ziploc bag with pills in it.

"I have a goody bag, too," I said as I reached in my pocket and pulled mine out. "That's cool," I said as if I needed anymore drugs in my life.

As we walked out she told her uncle that she loved him and locked the door. We rode in my car, and we went to a club downtown called Chicks Before Dicks. *Cool name*, I thought as we pulled up.

"You'll like this spot," she said.

She grabbed my hand as we walked in. I felt funny when she grabbed my hand, but, as I looked around, I realized that just about everyone in there was coupled up. The studs in there looked just like boys. Some were tall and reminded me of Eric, and some were just plain sexy. We headed for the VIP area, and, there, she introduced me to the owner of the club. Her name was Cheryl, and she was a stud, as well. I thought, *Damn! Are there any women left who still like dick?*

"It's a pleasure to meet you," she said as she kissed the top of my hand. "You gals enjoy yourselves and have a good time."

Bianca was sexy, too, but I didn't know if I wanted to be on that level with her, or did I? Cheryl came back with a bottle of Hennessey.

"You must have read my mind," I said as I grabbed a glass.

"Great minds think alike," she said before she walked off.

"So, what do you want to do? Would you like to pop a pill or do some powder cocaine?"

Cocaine was out of the question. I hated the side effects. Plus, it brought back too many memories of when I was in the streets. When I was tricking in the streets, I had to have at least an eight ball of coke to get me through the night. I reached in my pocket and pulled out the bag that dumb and dumber had left.

"Let me see what you have there," she said as she reached for my bag.

"Oh, shit! You have double stacks in here. I can pop three of these and be good all night," she said as she threw them in her mouth.

"I'm going to fuck the shit out of somebody's daughter tonight."

It's not going to be me, I thought as I popped two of the pills.

"I've never tried pills before. How do they make you feel?"

"If you've never done them, then you probably should have just taken a half of one. They make me freaky," she said as she poured herself a shot of Hennessey.

"I don't need to get any freakier," I said as I popped two more.

We got up to dance, and everyone around me was starting to slowly fade away. I was hot, and I started to take off my clothes.

"That's what I'm talking about," Bianca said as I fell to the floor.

36
Just Say NO!

When I woke up, I was in a hospital bed with tubes in my nose and a room full of studs in my face. When I opened my eyes, I tried to get up, but I was chained to the bed.

"Girl, you scared us last night. You popped too many pills, and you almost died," Bianca said.

"You're lucky," the doctor said. "You made it to the hospital just in time for us to pump the pills out of your stomach."

"Where are my twins?" I slurred. "And why am I chained to the damn bed?"

"Standard procedure," the doctor said as he looked at his clipboard.

"How do you feel?" they both asked me.

"I still feel high, and I can't believe that I fell out."

The doctor said, "Young people today are doing all types of drugs to get high. My advice to you, young lady, is to just say no!"

"Can you please take these damn handcuffs off me?" I said as I tried to sit up.

"The nurse will be in here shortly," he said.

The doctor left, but Bianca stayed by my side. The nurse came in and said, "You are anemic, so you need to take iron pills daily."

She, then, gave me my discharge papers.

"What does that mean? I feel like superwoman."

"It means that your blood is low, and these iron pills will help your blood. Just take these pills and follow up with your regular doctor in three days."

"Why am I still chained to the bed?"

"That's standard. We didn't know if you were suicidal or not."

"Well, I'm not," I said. "Now, can you please unhook me?"

Now, I knew how my brother felt with those damn shackles. I couldn't remember anything from last night, but I made up my mind that I would never pop another pill in my life. Bianca said that she was immune to those pills, so I gave her the whole bag. We got in my car, and she drove us to the Marriott downtown.

"This is what you need— some peace and quiet."

I agreed with her because I wasn't ready to face anyone else in my circle. I laid in the bed, and Bianca took her clothes off in front of me, and I saw she was wearing a big, brown strap on. She had on a wife beater and a pair of boxers. *Damn, she wants to be a boy for real. She's wearing a fake dick,* I thought. She took it off and got into the jacuzzi.

"The water feels fine," she said. "You can join me if you'd like."

She was crazy for wearing a fake dick, but, overall, she was cool. She had a nice shape. I thought most studs did. They wore baggy clothes to hide it. I checked my phone, and there were no missed calls. I laid there for a minute, debating whether or not I should join her. I took off of my clothes, revealing my hot pink panty and bra set.

"I know you're not gay, so we can just chill," she said as she helped me in.

"It's whatever," I said as I added more hot water.

"I see you like your water hot."

"Yes, I do. The hotter, the better," I said as I turned it off. "I'm glad that you were there for me."

"I'm glad I was too because nobody else would have gotten you to the hospital in time."

That felt good coming from her. I really felt that she was a true friend, and it didn't matter if she was gay or not.

"So, you have twins?" she asked as she looked at my flat stomach.

"Yes. Shelton and Sherita."

"Well, looking at your body, you don't look like you've had any kids at all."

"Thanks," I said as I splashed water in my face. "This is relaxation."

"Me and my ex used to come here a lot and get in the Jacuzzi, but that bitch was only using me to get discounts at Versace. I guess everybody has to play the fool sometimes."

"I say that exact same shit all the time," I said as I stared off into space. "Well, you'll be okay. There are a lot more fish in the sea."

"That's easy for you to say. You have it made."

"Right about now, I'd wear your shoes to get out of this bullshit that I'm in. I wouldn't have it made if Spencer knew the *real* me. He'd have my head on a platter."

"We all have secrets," she said as she popped a pill, "but I won't dwell on my ex too much. It's just that everywhere I go reminds me of her."

"Well, don't go where y'all used to go. Change up the scenery."

"You want a pill?" she joked.

"Hell, no, but I will take a glass of that fine wine."

"I'll get it for you," she said as she got up.

The water looked so good running down her body as she got up. She was so nice, and she treated me like Spencer did. I really thought that she was a boy trapped in a girl's body because she acted just like a boy.

"Here you are," she said as she got back in and handed me a glass of wine.

"So, I see you have a plastic dick. Do you wear that all the time?"

"Only when I go clubbing because, sometimes, anything goes in there. I probably would have got some pussy from somebody last night. Who knows? I saw some new femmes in there last night."

"Do you actually cum from fucking a girl with a fake dick?"

"Well, not exactly. That's just something I like to do. I know how to use my tongue and my fake dick."

"I didn't mean to offend you."

"Oh, you didn't offend me. I have bi-curious and straight girls who ask me all kinds of questions."

The more wine I drank, the more she was starting to look like a boy. She had the right size body structure. The muscles in her arm were just the right size, too.

"I might be bi-curious," I said as I flashed a nipple at her.

"Don't start anything that you can't finish or handle," she said as she twisted her dreads.

"Please. If I start anything, I will finish it," I said as I took off my bra and threw it across the room.

"Is that an invite?"

"It's whatever you want it to be," I said as I licked one of my hard nipples.

"Let me do that for you," she said as she came closer.

"No, I want to lick yours. You can be Bianca with me. Please stop acting like a boy," I said as I rubbed her dreads. "Why are you gay?"

"I've been gay all of my life."

"You are a pretty girl," I said as I looked into her eyes.

"I've always looked at girls in a sexual way. Boys never interested me."

"I thought you just woke up one morning and said, 'I want to be gay.' I'm just joking," I said.

I was tired of those plastic dicks. I wanted to feel her warm tongue on my pussy. She came closer to me and put both of my breasts together and licked them at the same time. My clit jumped, and I grabbed her face and started kissing her. Her tongue was so warm, and her skin next to mine felt even better.

"Are you sure you want to do this?" she asked as we continued to kiss.

"I'm doing it, aren't I?"

"You know. Once I put that dick on you, you're going to be calling me every day."

"That's just it. I don't want that fake ass dick. I want your warm tongue."

"Why not get both?" she said. "I could double the pleasure."

"No, thanks," I said as I got out of the jacuzzi and headed for the bed.

"My tongue is more powerful than my dick is," she said as she followed me to the bed.

"Well, that's a risk that I will have to take."

I slid off my panties and laid there for her to have her way with me.

"Are you sure that this is what you want to do?"

"Girl, bring your ass here," I said. "And, yes, I'm sure."

We started to kiss again, and she licked me from my head to my toe. She stopped and went to the mini kitchen to get some ice cubes. She put the ice in her mouth while she was licking on my nipples. And the feeling was a good sensation. It felt so good. I was reaching to grab her, but she was in a zone. Then, she made her way down to my pussy. She was sliding the ice in and out between my pussy lips. She was slurping and licking my clit so fast. It was like her tongue had batteries! *This is how those girls get turned out,* I thought. This was definitely a feeling that I could get used to. I had never eaten pussy before, and I wasn't about to. I felt my clit getting hard, and I was about to cum. I needed to relieve some stress.

"Oh, that's it! Right there, baby," I said as I moved her head faster.

I was fucking her face hard because I was about to release and unwind. I finally came, and she didn't stop licking me. I came again and again. Multiple orgasms were the best. She came up for air, and we both looked at the ceiling, breathing hard.

"I told you I could work my tongue," she said.

"You sure can," I said as I kissed her, smelling my pussy on her breath.

"So, how are you going to get satisfied?" I asked.

"I am satisfied because I made you feel good, and that's my satisfaction."

"You mean to tell me that you don't want me to play with your pussy or nothing?"

"Nope. I just want you to promise me that you'll let me satisfy you more often."

37
Back to Life

When I got back to my loft, I just wanted to lay down in my bed all day.

"Bianca really let me have it, and she sure could work that tongue," I said with a smile.

She insisted that I call her "B" while she was satisfying me. I wanted to chill the whole day alone. Right when I was about to turn on the TV, the phone rang, and it was Eric. I didn't know if I should answer it because he hadn't called me until then. Finally, I answered, and he said, "What's up? I've been looking for you. Where have you been?"

"I was out with a few friends," I said, rolling my neck at the phone like he was right there in my face.

I didn't want to be with him anymore. He really let me know that he didn't care about me. I wanted to call this shit off before Spencer found out.

"I'm on the way," he said before hanging up.

I called Spencer's cell phone, and there was still no answer. I wondered if he had gone out of town. He never told me any of his business, and I didn't want to know. I went to run myself a hot bubble bath. I thought, *How am I going to break up with Eric?* There was a chance that that would have been the start of World War III, but the shit had to stop.

"Look, Eric. This isn't going to work," I said as I practiced my speech in the mirror.

That wouldn't work. Maybe I should tell him while I was riding him. Hell, no! He'd kill me.

"What will I say?" I asked as I slid down the bathroom wall onto the floor.

I knew, for a fact, that I wanted it to be over, but how? So far, I felt that I'd gotten away with murder. Murder? That was it. Maybe, I should kill his ass. I slid off my clothes and settled into the steamy water. I was in the mood to listen to some music. Although rap was my thing, I had the blues, and I wanted to listen to some of Spencer's oldies. I saw why Spencer listened to those songs. They had meaning behind them. Those songs were calming, and each one told a story. I put on one of Johnnie Taylor's CDs. *This is what I need to listen to,* I thought as I let the steamy water caress my bones. Just as I was standing up and singing in the mirror, Eric came in and turned off the music.

"We need to talk."

"About what?"

"I am broke, and I need some more money."

"What have you been doing with all of the money that I have been giving you?"

"I gambled it all away, and I owe a very dangerous man some money. If I don't pay him off, he's going to kill me."

This couldn't be more perfect, I thought to myself. If someone killed his ass, then I would be in the clear.

"So, what are you saying? How much money do you need from me?"

"About twenty thousand."

"Twenty thousand dollars? Boy, are you crazy?"

He walked over to my DVD player and put in the sex tape that he had recorded.

"It would be a shame if Unk saw this. This would probably give the old man a heart attack," he said as he turned the volume up.

I watched as I was riding him and biting on his ears.

"This is my insurance, and I will hold onto this until you get me that twenty thousand dollars. If I show this to him, he will kill you just like he did Jo Ann. Everyone knows that he killed her and got rid of her body. If you must know the whole truth and nothing but the truth, the whole NBA shit was just a hoax. I had everyone fooled, including my so-called mother. I am a gambler, and, if you must know, I am in over my head. I will bet on anything from football games to horse races. You win some, and you lose some, and I have lost up to my neck, and that's where you come in. You will get me that money, and, by the way, Q is locked up. He tried to buy a gun from a dealer who knows Spencer. The dealer came back and told Spencer, and, because Q is a three-time felon, Spencer made it so Q will never see light again, so that was the end of Q. Just thought maybe you wanted to know that, so I am the only threat you have. No harm will come to the old man as long as you give me what I ask for when I ask for it!"

"Eric, how could you do this to me? I thought you said that you loved me?"

"How could I love a bitch who is married and fucked me on the first day," he cold-heartedly said. "You didn't even know me, and, besides, you were an easy target. So, if I were you, I'd think about the future of those twins."

"But, Eric, I love you," I said as I sat on the sofa, continuing to watch the video of us.

I couldn't stop the tears from coming down my face. My heart felt like it had been torn out of my chest. I knew deep down inside that he didn't really love me, but I thought that he respected me, considering all the shit that I had done for him. I was thinking that I could just shoot him, claim he was an intruder, and get it over with, but that wouldn't work. My name was on his bills. Not to mention, he was driving my Bentley all over town.

"I know you don't think that I love you," he said as he ejected the disc.

"How do I know that that is the only copy, and that you didn't make more?"

"You just have to take my word for it," he said as he put the disc in his pocket. "Everything will be just fine if you do what I say. I won't show this to Spencer as long as you cough up the dough as needed."

I had to think of a plan and think of it quick. If I could get twenty thousand dollars, it would be used to murder Eric's ass.

38
In the Midst

I dried my tears and looked at myself in the mirror and said, "I am from the streets. I will go to G-Man's spot and pay one of them to kill Eric."

Since Spencer was out of town, that day was the perfect time to go and grab the cash. I had to think of a plan and think of one quick before the shit hit the fan. I walked in and unlocked the door and found a house full of people, including Spencer. He was having some type of party, and, as I looked around, I saw that they were all well-dressed men in suits. Then, I saw a banner that read "Welcome Home, Fred".

"Sweetie, you're just in time," Spencer said as he grabbed my hand. "This is one of my best friends. His name is Fred, and he just finished a fifteen year bid."

"So, you're the lovely young lady that has my friend's nose wide open," Fred said as he kissed the top of my hand.

Just what I needed— another old ass man kissing on me. I looked around, but I didn't see any familiar faces. The only person that I knew in there was Walter. He smiled and nodded his head. I really didn't feel like chatting with Spencer and his buddies. I thought, *Now is a good time to go sneak out in the shed and see who he and Rita are hiding.* I excused myself from Spencer and his buddies. I walked down the long foyer to look for Rita and the twins, but there was no sign of them. I walked to the back door, and I was happy. I was finally going to see what or who was in the shed. Then, as I opened the door, I heard laughter, and I saw Rita and the twins.

"There you guys are," I said as I played it off like I was looking for them.

"So, why aren't you in there?" Rita asked as she looked back at the shed.

"I just told you that I was looking for you guys. Besides, I missed my twins," I said as I rolled my eyes at her.

"Mommy! Mommy! We saw the scary lady," the twins said as they looked back at the shed.

"What scary lady?" I asked as I looked at Rita.

"What did I tell you guys? This is our little secret," Rita said as she looked at them.

"Remember the scary lady from the movie that we watched last night. We watched a movie called *The Exorcist* last night, and they were scared of the lady on there."

I looked at her and saw that she was lying straight through her teeth. I went along with it by saying, "Oh, yeah, you mean the lady whose head turned all the way around?"

"Mommy, her head didn't turn all the way around," Shelton said.

My twins were five years old, and they knew the difference between real life and TV, but I went on with the lie that Rita said. I was going to go in that shed if I had to knock her ass out cold!

"Who wants some chocolate chip cookies?" Rita asked.

"We do! We do!" the twins said at the same time.

I didn't know how dumb she thought I was, but I was going in that shed. As I walked back in, Spencer's company was leaving. I was glad because I didn't want to put on any more fake smiles. After Spencer saw his company off, he asked me how I had been enjoying my space.

"I like it," I said.

I didn't know if he was on to Eric and me or not, but I wasn't going to tell on myself. I didn't care how many questions he asked me or how suspicious he became.

"I know that you're a young girl, and you want to club and show off your new rides, too. That's why I have allowed you to have so much free time. I know you don't want me crowding your space. I trust you, and I know that you will never cheat on me," he said as he kissed my hand.

I felt a few sweat bubbles pop up on my head as I looked at him, looking me dead in my eyes with a serious look.

"You look tense," Spencer said as he walked over and rubbed my shoulders. "Is everything okay?"

"Sure. Why wouldn't everything be okay?" I said as I walked over to fix myself a drink. "I have everything a girl could possibly want."

I started naming things and felt like I was about to break down at the same time.

"I am out of the ghetto. My kids have a super nanny. I married a rich man who has given me the world. What could I possibly be tense about?" I said as I turned the bottle of Hennessey up. "I have George on my mind, and he's probably why I am looking so down. He has to do seven years."

"Oh, I've been meaning to tell you about that. He's been convicted of the rape charge, and he, now, has to do a total of twenty years."

"What! How could that be possible?"

"Your brother has a rap sheet that is longer than your arm and my arm put together."

"I have to go see him and let him know. He's not going to be able to do all of that hard time alone."

"Oh, and about that visitation. He has been transferred to a federal prison in Washington."

"When were you going to tell me?"

"I was going to tell you when the time was right."

"Oh, so you didn't think that the time was right yesterday or whenever you found out? Spencer, how could you keep something like this from me?"

"Your brother has done some things that will probably cost him his life."

"What do you mean 'cost him his life'?"

"What I mean is, he could die in prison, or he could kill someone in there and get the electric chair. Who knows? Anything goes behind bars."

"I can't believe that you can't get him out of prison. Can you at least get him out for a week?"

"No, I'm afraid not. The choices that we make in life have to be thought through very carefully," he said as he stared at me.

"This is my only family we're talking about. I don't have a mother or a daddy, and, now, you're telling me that my brother, who has looked out for me all my life, will be spending the next twenty years of his life in prison in fucking Washington D.C.! How am I supposed to feel?"

I was so mad at Spencer. And the way he said things didn't make the situation any better. He, suddenly, became very cold, and the look that he had on his face let me know that he didn't have any sympathy for my brother George. I told Spencer that I was going for a ride to clear my mind. I had to get to that safe and get some money out, so I could eliminate my problems one by one. He looked at me with a strange look on his face and said, "Ride on. I'm not going anywhere. I will be right here when you get back with your clear mind."

Spencer put on "Who's Making Love" by Johnnie Taylor as I left.

I needed a miracle.

I wanted to call Eric and see if we could come to some type of agreement. I wasn't able to get in the safe and grab any cash. When I thought about it, I probably would have been happier living in the ghetto than I was living in that mansion with my life on the line. I wasn't afraid to die, but I didn't want to die by Spencer's hands. No one knew where Spencer's wife was, but I thought that I had an idea. I believed that she was in the shed, but what if she wasn't, and I was wrong. But the twins said that they had seen a scary lady, and, if she'd been kidnapped for ten years, then she'd probably look scary. I didn't know what to think. I needed cash, and I couldn't get it. I needed my brother, and he was gone. I needed God himself to show up and get me out of the mess that I was in. I needed a miracle and, from the looks of it, it was on 34th Street, and I didn't know where the hell that was. I had a couple of tricks up my sleeve, though. If Eric wanted to play dirty, then so could I. My mother's name was Twinkie, and she never took shit from any niggas. I had the perfect plan. I was going to set up a robbery between Eric and G-Man. I didn't care who got killed. They could blow each other up for all I cared.

I called Eric and told him to meet me at my place. I told him that I had the perfect way for him to get millions of dollars and drugs. I called G-Man and described Eric to him. I told him that Eric would try to rob him. They both fell for it. When Eric came to my house, I wanted to get one last fuck in. He was so arrogant. If he had played his cards right, maybe I'd have let him breathe. I was starting to think like my brother George. He didn't care, if someone was a problem, he killed their ass with the quickness.

"What's the plan?" Eric said as he walked in.

"The plan is simple, baby. I know where a lot of drugs and cash are. You can pay your debt and then some, but, first, can you please give me some of that good-ass dick?"

I didn't even bother to look out the door to see if he had a bitch in my car. At that point, I didn't care, and it didn't matter. He was going to be dead within twenty-four hours. The plan was for them to see him drive up to the drive thru window in my car. Then, they were going to ambush him with bullets. *I really hate that this good dick has to go rot in the grave, but he's leaving me no choice.* I didn't want Spencer dead, but, if Eric would have come up with a plan for us to kill Spencer and be together, I probably would have gone along with it, but he showed me that he didn't want me at all. So, when he went to G-Man's spot, he'd get exactly what he deserved.

For some strange reason, I felt in my heart that Spencer had something to do with more time being added to George's sentence.

"Where is this spot at?" Eric said as he pulled off his clothes.

"It's on Bankhead, not too far from Bankhead Seafood. It's the big house that sits next to the church with the big, black fence around it. You can't miss it. No one will be there, and all you have to do is drive to the back and go in the back window."

"How do you know what's in there?"

"I know because my friend named Keisha has a boyfriend who is a big time drug dealer."

"If I wasn't desperate, I wouldn't be doing this," he said as he got under the covers with me.

"Well, sometimes, a boy's got to do what a boy's got to do."

He kissed me and said, "When this is all over, I have something to tell you."

What could he possibly want to tell me? Well, whatever it was it would have to wait until I was reunited with him in hell because his ass was going to die. I got on top of him and rode his dick. He held me so tight. It was almost like he was really trying to make love to me and not fuck me. It definitely felt different. When he finished, he reminded me that, when this was all over, he'd tell me the whole truth.

"Now, I got to go and get this money," he said as he put on his clothes.

I walked him to the door, and, sure enough, a bitch was driving my car.

"Smooches," I said as I closed the door. I called G-Man to let him know that Eric was en route.

39
What Have I Done?

Eric went over there, and they sprayed my Bentley up with bullets. Eric was dead just like that. I was sad in a way, but I was relieved because Spencer would never see the disc. When I arrived at Spencer's, he was crying, and Evelyn was crying, too.

"Why are y'all looking like someone has just died?" I asked as I closed the door.

"Eric's dead," Evelyn said, "and I want to know why he was in your car at that drug house? Spencer, I told you I had a bad vibe about this young-ass bitch."

She blew her nose.

"Sweetheart, Eric is dead, and we want some answers," Spencer said.

"I don't have any answers. He said that he wanted to drive my car because it was fast. How was I supposed to know he was going to commit a robbery?"

"You better tell me something, bitch, before I kill your ass!" Evelyn shouted. "My only son is dead!"

"He's not even your son," I said as I looked at Spencer. "Eric told me that he was adopted and that you weren't even his real uncle."

"Bitch, if you don't stop lying on my son, I will come over there and choke the life out of your married, sneaky black ass! I was in labor for twenty-two hours with him. He is my fucking son. I shitted him out my ass. Now, what will I do?"

"Wait a minute. You mean to tell me that you didn't see him playing basketball at a park?"

"Hell, no. What damn park? What the fuck are you talking about?"

"Eric told me that Spencer saw him playing basketball at a park, and he saw that he had the potential to be in the NBA."

"Bitch, are you crazy? My son is not adopted! And I suppose he also told you that he saw Spencer kill his wife, too? Eric was seven years old when that happened, and Spencer was very careful. He made sure that no one saw him on that night."

Oh, my God! What have I done? Spencer did kill her! I was pissing on myself and didn't know it until I felt something warm coming down my legs.

"What's wrong?" Spencer said as he tapped me on my shoulder with a wicked look on his face. "You look like you've just seen a ghost."

Spencer was a killer! Oh, my God! What if Eric was going to tell me that he really wasn't going to tell Spencer about us? What if he really did owe some loan sharks? What if he really did love me? I was starting to feel like I was about to die. Why did he lie to me about being adopted? It just didn't make any sense.

"Where are my twins?" I asked Spencer.

"Oh, they are somewhere safe. I'm going to take Evelyn home, and I'll be back. We have some business to talk about."

"I want to see my twins," I said as I started to cry.

I didn't have either one of my guns with me. I was shit out of luck. When Spencer walked out the door, I ran to the twins' room, and they were gone. I called their names throughout the house and still heard no sign of them. I was scared to go to the shed now because I didn't want to know who or what was in there. I didn't care. I wanted my twins and myself to get out of this ordeal alive. I took a deep breath and started to walk towards the kitchen. Shelton came flying in, saying, "Mommy! Mommy, the scary lady has Sherita!"

"Wait a minute! Calm down! What scary lady? Where is this scary lady?"

"The scary lady was in the shed, and she got Rita, and she has Sherita, too. Mommy, I ran so fast! She's coming in here, and she was dragging Rita by her head."

He was terrified, and I was too. I had already pissed on myself, and, if I saw Spencer's wife come alive from the dead, I'd probably shit on myself.

"Mommy, the scary lady said that she wasn't going to hurt us. She said that she wanted Spencer."

"Well, Shelton, what does she look like? Where is she?"

"I'm right here," I heard a woman's voice say.

40
Am I Dreaming?

As I turned around, I saw Rita, lying on the floor, unconsciousness, and I slowly looked at the woman who had her by the head.

"Lady, I'm sorry that your husband held you back there for all those years. I don't even love him. I only want him for his money," I said not wanting to look at her face. "We can kill him together. Can you please tell me where you hid my daughter? Did you kill my daughter? Please tell me that you didn't take a child's life."

I was so afraid to look at her.

"I didn't kill your daughter. I locked her in a closet downstairs, and I would have caught this little bastard, but he runs too fast! And I am not Spencer's wife."

"Then, who are you?" I said as I slowly looked her in her face. "Twinkie!"

"Tameka!"

She dropped Rita's head and ran and hugged me.

"Mama, you mean to tell me that you're not dead?"

We looked at each other and cried. We looked identical. I looked exactly like her.

"Wait a minute, Mama! You have been back there for all those years? What did you do for him to keep you back there? Mama, where is my daughter? What closet did you lock her in? Shelton, go and get her."

"She is in the closet downstairs by the foyer. When I saw these kids, I didn't know that they were my grandkids running around and playing in the back. I would see them through that small window and just watch them run freely while Rita threw me leftover scraps."

"But how did you get out? I had a feeling that someone was back there. I tried to come back there so many times, but I never had the chance. Spencer or Rita has always caught me. Well, why did he keep you alive? What did you do to him? Oh, my God! I married him, and he killed his first wife. I can't prove it, but I know he did."

"I can prove it. Her remains are in the shed. I used to work for Spencer, but he was so controlling, so, one day, I got tired of his shit. I stole fifteen million dollars from him."

"But why didn't he kill you? Why did he keep you alive?"

"He didn't kill me because this bitch right here is my sister," she said as she kicked Rita by the head.

"What! This is my auntie, and she knew that my mother wasn't dead! Mama, I love you so much. I am so glad that you're alive. I am so confused, though."

"You shouldn't be," Rita said as Twinkie held her head. "I was the sister that always got the shitty end of the stick."

"But you're Mexican, and we're black," I said as I hugged Sherita as she ran into my arms.

"We have different daddies," Twinkie interrupted.

"I still don't understand. The plan was for Spencer to kill you, and we would live happily ever after. He wanted to kill you along with Twinkie, and we would raise the twins. You see that I never hurt them. I love them. They're my great-niece and nephew," she said as she walked over to my twins.

"Bitch, if you touch my grandkids, I will drop you where you stand," Twinkie said.

"I am still confused. What the fuck do you mean 'you and Spencer will live happily ever after'?"

Rita decided to tell the whole story.

"It was no accident that Spencer came to your rescue when you broke down in that car that Ethel had given you. It was all a set-up, and he staged the drug raid, so Bernard would go to jail forever. He killed your friend Keisha, too."

"What she means is that she was a backstabbing-ass bitch. She was supposed to be Jo Ann's best friend, but she was sleeping with Spencer," Twinkie said. "Jo Ann cut Spencer's dick off when she found out, and they both killed her. I took fifteen million dollars from Spencer because he was not paying me fairly, so I saw an opportunity and took it. It just so happens that my so-called best friend Ethel told on me."

"You mean Old Lady Ethel from the projects? No wonder she was always so nice to me. She felt guilty."

"Twinkie, I kept you alive for all these years. Can you please let me get some money out of the safe and leave town? I don't want to go down for Jo Ann's murder," Rita pleaded.

I walked over to Rita and slapped her and said, "That's for getting smart with me all those times when you did."

I slapped her again and said, "Bitch, that's for keeping my fucking mama away from me after all these years. I should knock your fucking teeth out."

I pushed her to the floor.

"Sister, do you want to tell her about George, or should I do the honors?" Rita said as she licked her blood from her bleeding lip.

"I'll tell her bitch. Sweetheart, George is your daddy. And I didn't want you to know of him because he was so damn crazy. There. Happy?" Twinkie said as she looked at Rita.

"I'm sorry, but I was going to get that fifteen million dollars and come back for you and George, but Spencer found out and kidnapped me."

"He's my what?"

"I was going to tell you once we had gotten out of here. Spencer is a very dangerous man, and he will kill anybody that gets in his way."

No wonder George took such good care of me. He was my fucking daddy, but, the last time I went to see him in jail, I found out that he had been moved to another prison and that he was going to do twenty years!

"So, you mean to tell me that the man I thought was my brother is my damn daddy? Why didn't he tell me?"

"Because he made a promise to me that he would keep his mouth closed."

No wonder I didn't give a fuck about shit because he was crazy as hell. I didn't know how to feel, but I definitely wanted him to get out of jail.

"I promise you guys that I will help get your little fucking dysfunctional family back together again," Rita said. "Please just hear me out, Twinkie. I don't want to go to jail. I'm sorry for keeping you back there for all those years."

"Bitch, you just told us that you and Spencer were going to kill me and my daughter and raise my grandkids. Why should I trust you?"

"You should trust me, sister, because I have proof."

"And, bitch, your proof is what?"

"I can help you get George out of jail."

I was so relieved that both of my parents were alive, but that still didn't stop the rotten soul I had inside of me. I was the daughter of a gangster and a drug dealer.

"Let's walk down the hall to my room," Rita said as she got up from the floor. She went to her closet and pulled out a box and said, "This is the proof that some of George's charges were false. Here is a copy of the staged drug raid for Bernard."

She handed me the sheet of paper explaining the raid on my apartment that had put Bernard in jail. I didn't care about him. He could rot in jail for all I cared, so I tore up the evidence.

"Oh, yeah! This is the fake policy of fifty million dollars," Rita said.

"What! I got fucked by plastic dicks for nothing?" I said as I looked at the paper. I laughed and said, "That's why I fucked his nephew and let him eat my pussy afterwards."

"You did what?" Twinkie said. "Well, you got it honest."

"Spencer doesn't have a dick, so I fucked his fine-ass nephew."

"By the way, Spencer knew about him, too," Rita said.

"Well, I'm glad he knew, and I don't give a fuck. The policy is fake, and Eric is dead. I got Eric killed."

"You got someone else killed," Rita said. "It wasn't Eric. Eric wasn't a fool. He was young, but he wasn't dumb. He sent his friend Rodney over there."

"Eric is alive."

"Yes, I am alive," he said as he walked in and hugged me. "I sent that nigga Rodney over there because he was in on the plot to kill you with Spencer."

"Oh, my God! I am so happy. I am so sorry. Eric, please forgive me. I was so scared that Spencer was going to kill me if he found out about us."

"No, can you please forgive me?" he said as he kissed me. "That was my uncle's doing, and I didn't mean to hurt you, but he was so controlling, and he had my mind, so I did what he told me to do. And when he killed you, he wanted to make you look like a complete gold digger. He already has the whole town fooled by having everyone think that he didn't kill Jo Ann, but, baby, I do love you," he said as he looked at his watch.

"Not so fast," Spencer said as he pointed an AK-47 semi-automatic at us. "All of you, line your asses up against the wall."

I thought, *We should have gotten out of the house instead of having a fucking family reunion.* But it was too late. All the dirt I had ever done in my life was flashing in my head.

"You get over there, too," he said as he pointed the gun at Rita.

No one said anything. I was silently praying.

"Spencer, this is between me and you. Why did you have to bring my daughter into this?" Twinkie said.

"Because I am a man who gets what I want. You took my money, and I was going to take your daughter. No one takes anything from me. I am Spencer Raymond Davis," he said as he beat himself on his chest. "So, which one of you fucks want to die first? Nephew, you look pretty good for a dead man."

He pointed the rifle at him.

"I know all about you fucking my wife. I knew that you were driving the cars that I bought her. You were supposed to dog her out, not fall in love with the pussy. I got all of those tickets where you ran red lights! I have photos of you in the driver seat. You weren't supposed to fuck her. You were supposed to trick her, so I could get away with murder a second time. And if I had known you were going to be a threat, I would have killed your ass when you were just seven years old when I killed Jo Ann. Or maybe I should kill my sneaky-ass wife first. She has fucked everyone in town, including my best friend Walter. She fucked you. She fucked girls that she didn't know. I know all about you and your sneaky ways, you money hungry bitch, but I wanted you to do all of those things, so, when I pulled this trigger, my dick would be hard."

"But you don't got a dick. You mean your plastic dick," I said as I held my twins closer to me. Right when he aimed the rifle at me, I saw a red dot on his forehead, then I heard a gunshot. I felt warm blood all over my face. Spencer fell to the ground, and Eric grabbed me.

"Are you okay?" Eric asked.

"I don't know. Am I dead?"

"No, you're not dead. Before I came over here, I called the police, and I put on this wire for the police to hear everything on tape. Luckily, Spencer confessed to Jo Ann's murder," he said as he pulled up his shirt.

All the cops came in and swarmed the place.

"I'm sorry, ma'am, but you're going down for the murder of Jo Ann Davis," a cop said as he handcuffed Rita.

"For what it's worth, I'm sorry," Rita said as she walked out with her head down.

I wanted to kiss Eric's six pack.

"You saved our lives, and I tried to take yours."

"I understand why you wanted to. I put you through a lot," he said as he kicked the rifle away from Spencer's hand.

"Good job, young man," an officer said as he shook Eric's hand.

"What took y'all so long? We were scared as hell in here."

"No need to be scared. We had sharp shooters all over this place."

"So, what's next?" I asked Twinkie.

"We're going to dig up my fifteen million dollars."

"I'm going to check the safe," I said as I ran out. I opened up the safe and there was nothing in there but a note that read, *"I will see you in hell you married, sneaky, black bitch."*

41
There is a God

We got in my Maybach and drove to the field where Twinkie had buried the fifteen million dollars. She had buried the money at a park called Anderson Park on the West Side. When Eric was done digging, he pulled up a Louis Vuitton suitcase that had all crisp twenty dollar bills in it.

I was glad that Twinkie was alive and that she had hid the money because I didn't get any money from Spencer. She didn't raise me, but I wasn't mad at her at all. She felt that she had to do what she had to do, and I had to do what I had to do.

We got George out of jail. He said that he was going to tell me that I was his daughter when the time was right. He also told me that he knew that I was a tough cookie because I had his and Twinkie's blood running in my veins. He also told me that he knew that Spencer was dangerous. That was why he wanted to get out of jail and kill him so badly. I didn't judge him because we all did things that we didn't want to do. I loved him and Twinkie even more just for having me.

I had even arranged for Q to get out of jail. We had started out on the wrong foot, but we eventually became like family. Spencer had killed Jo Ann, and she was his mother, and I felt sorry for him. I couldn't bring her back, but I could make his life easier by getting him out of jail.

I kept my cars, but I didn't want the mansion that Spencer had died in. There were just too many bad memories there. It was worth forty million dollars, but I sold it for thirty million.

I was entitled to it since I was legally his wife, but I didn't want to live in it. Evelyn wasn't mad at me anymore once she found out that Eric was alive.

It turned out that Spencer was the adopted one. He and Evelyn weren't blood after all. So, technically, I didn't sleep with his nephew. Twinkie said that she had always dreamed of living by the beach. She said she always saw herself sipping margaritas on the beach. I didn't care where we moved as long as we were together. She finally broke down and told me why she and Rita were rival sisters. She said that Rita had been jealous of her ever since they were teenagers. She explained to me that Rita was mad at her because she was the smart one in school.

"Everything I had as a child, she wanted. If I had a black Barbie doll, then she wanted a black Barbie doll. She was always so competitive with me. And as you saw, she was the one with the long, pretty hair, and I was the one with the brains. I didn't want to be like our mother and live paycheck to paycheck. I ran the streets, and I literally ran them, too."

I stopped her and said, "We all have a past, so let's just leave it in the past."

I was starting to sound like Spencer, but I didn't want to be reminded of my past, nor did I want to talk about it.

She hugged me and said, "I will take care of you and my grandkids. George and I will have fun being grandparents."

She looked at Shelton and Sherita. George was ten years younger than her. I couldn't believe that I had thought he was my brother. They had really had me fooled.

Twinkie wanted us to move to California, and we did just that, and she opened up a night club. It was called T & T. It stood for Twinkie and Tameka. The palm trees were so nice out there. I wondered if God was going to punish me for all the dirt that I'd done, but everyone in my circle had done dirt. *Only God can judge me,* I thought. I didn't want to go back to Atlanta —

period. I wanted to leave that fucked up past where it was and start a fresh new life with Eric.

Twinkie didn't raise me but I didn't see why we couldn't start off with a fresh clean slate. She could be a grandmother to the twins. It was never too late for that.

Twinkie bought a mansion in the California hills, and Eric and I purchased one right next door to hers. I thought, *There is a God. He answered my prayers and let me and my twins make it out of this crazy situation alive.* God had even done some extra stuff. He gave me my parents and a young man who I had a great deal of love for. And I found out that Twinkie and I had one more thing in common — we liked our men young.

About The Author

Antoinette Tunique Smith was born in San Francisco, California and raised in ATL, where she still resides. She is blessed with five children who are known as the five lights of her life: Pinky, Driah, Clyde, Chicken and Fat Boy.

She would like people to know that it doesn't matter where you come from, you can be whatever you wanna be. Just believe in God. There is a God!

Thanks &
Much respect,
Antoinette Smith

www.straighttothepointbooks.com

acansing2000@yahoo.com

www.straighttothepointbooks.com

acansing2000@yahoo.com

CPSIA information can be obtained
at www.ICGtesting.com
Printed in the USA
FSHW021839130521
81311FS